MIDNIGHT AMBUSH

Rough hands grabbed him in the darkness, and a voice said, "You're about to take your last steps, Mr. Newspaper Editor. Take your medicine like a man."

Will Jones ducked, whirled and ran into the night. Gunfire came from behind him. Two shots. Another. Three more. A bullet whined off a rock near his feet. Another pulled at the left side of his shirt.

Then the ground suddenly dropped from under him, and he was falling. Something exploded in his head, a bright light flashing through his brain. Then blackness covered him—blackness that was darker than the night.

THE UNTAMED WEST
brought to you by Zebra Books

THE LAST MOUNTAIN MAN   (1480, $2.25)
by William W. Johnstone
He rode out West looking for the men who murdered his father
and brother. When an old mountain man taught him how to kill a
man a hundred different ways from Sunday, he knew he'd make
sure they all remembered . . . THE LAST MOUNTAIN MAN.

SAN LOMAH SHOOTOUT   (1853, $2.50)
by Doyle Trent
Jim Kinslow didn't even own a gun, but a group of hardcases
tried to turn him into buzzard meat. There was only one way to
find out why anybody would want to stretch his hide out to dry,
and that was to strap on a borrowed six-gun and ride to death or
glory.

TOMBSTONE LODE   (1915, $2.95)
by Doyle Trent
When the Josey mine caved in on Buckshot Dobbs, he left behind
a rich vein of Colorado gold—but no will. James Alexander,
hired to investigate Buckshot's self-proclaimed blood relations
learns too soon that he has one more chance to solve the mystery
and save his skin or become another victim of TOMBSTONE
LODE.

GALLOWS RIDERS   (1934, $2.50)
by Mark K. Roberts
When Stark and his killer-dogs reached Colby, all it took was a
little muscle and some well-placed slugs to run roughshod over
the small town—until the avenging stranger stepped out of the
shadows for one last bloody showdown.

DEVIL WIRE   (1937, $2.50)
by Cameron Judd
They came by night, striking terror into the hearts of the settlers.
The message was clear: Get rid of the devil wire or the land would
turn red with fencestringer blood. It was the beginning of a brutal
range war.

*Available wherever paperbacks are sold, or order direct from the
Publisher. Send cover price plus 50¢ per copy for mailing and
handling to Zebra Books, Dept. 2071, 475 Park Avenue South,
New York, N.Y. 10016. Residents of New York, New Jersey and
Pennsylvania must include sales tax. DO NOT SEND CASH.*

DOYLE TRENT

TREACHERY TOWN

ZEBRA BOOKS
KENSINGTON PUBLISHING CORP.

ZEBRA BOOKS

are published by

Kensington Publishing Corp.
475 Park Avenue South
New York, NY 10016

First printing: May 1987

Printed in the United States of America

Chapter One

He didn't expect to be met by a brass band the first time he stepped inside the office of *The Maxwell Times*, but neither did he expect to find a girl with a gun.

She was nervous, scared. Her hands were trembling. "Who are you? What do you want?"

The bore of the gun looked to be as big as an open barn door, and he stopped so suddenly he almost tripped over his feet.

"What do you want?" She held the big single action revolver in both hands, pointed at the center of his chest. The gun was fully loaded with lead bullets, probably .44-40s.

Cold fear gripped him as he realized it took only a small pull on the trigger to send a heavy slug tearing into him. He tried to talk but could only croak:

"D—don't shoot. I, uh . . ."

He could see fear in her face too, a dark-complexioned face with high cheekbones and wide-spaced brown eyes. She was just as scared as he.

"Be . . . be careful with that." He knew her fear

made her more dangerous than a cold, calculating killer.

Then he noticed that the hammer was down. The gun wasn't cocked. She would have to pull the hammer back to shoot, and she apparently didn't know it.

Realizing that brought a heavy sigh of relief. His shoulders relaxed. He tried to smile. "Listen miss, my name is William C. Jones. Nathan Benchley was my uncle."

"Oh." Her hands were still trembling, but the gun was lowered a few inches.

"Would you like to see some identification, a letter addressed to me?"

"Uh, no." Slowly the gun was lowered until it was pointed at the floor. "I don't think that will be necessary. Are you really William Jones?"

"Yes miss, ma'am, miss."

"It's miss." She placed the gun carefully on an old rolltop desk in the corner of the long room. "I'm sorry about this, Mr. Jones. We've had a robbery here." She smiled, but weakly.

Her plain cotton dress came down to her lace-up shoes, and a narrow belt pulled the dress in at the waist. She was slender.

Will Jones came on into the room and looked around. What he saw was disappointing. The old desk had a leg missing, and it had been replaced by a short piece of firewood. The floor was wood, splintery, but swept clean.

In back of the desk was a flatbed press with a three-foot-high cylinder mounted over one end, and beyond that was a keyboard mono-typesetter. Cases of type faces were mounted on a heavy wooden table. After

6

seeing the presses at the Kansas City newspaper, he expected to find bigger equipment.

"Is this all?" He looked back at the girl. She appeared to be in her middle twenties. Her hair was dark but not coal black. It was parted in the middle and, except for a bow around her ears, it hung straight down to her shoulders. "Is this all the equipment my uncle had?"

"Yes, Mr. Jones, it is. And," she added, pointing at the desk, "someone broke in and took everything out of Mr. Benchley's desk. That's why I grabbed that . . . the gun when you came in. I'm sorry. You startled me."

"I apologize. I didn't mean to scare you."

"It's Jacob Mahoney's gun. He left a few minutes ago and left the gun on the desk."

"Jacob Mahoney?"

"He's the printer. I'm Marybelle Dubois, his helper. We worked for Mr. Benchley."

Somehow, from the dark color of her skin, he expected broken English to come from her, but instead her voice was well modulated, clear.

"Are there other employees?"

"No sir. We three put out the paper. Mr. Benchley did all the writing and editing."

"Why would anyone want to steal things from Uncle Nathan's desk? Did he have anything valuable in it?"

"We don't think he had anything in it but his papers, but we're not sure. We never touched it until Jake found the door pried open and the desk drawers rifled."

"Is anything missing that you know of?"

7

"Only his papers and some back issues of *The Times*. We told all this to the marshal, Mr. Vaughn, and he can't understand it either."

"Um." He studied the floor a moment, looking down on it from his height of six foot three. While he was doing that, she studied him, taking in his fedora hat, the dark coat worn over a gray vest, and the gray wool pants which had once been sharply creased down the front but were now wrinkled from four days of travel. A quick frown appeared and disappeared when she noticed the black, patent-leather shoes.

Will Jones was twenty-six, and he hoped his thick brown moustache made him look older. He was given to thinness, and like many thin men, he had a tendency to let his shoulders droop.

"You say a Mr. Mahoney is, was, Uncle Nathan's printer?"

"Yes sir."

"Where might I find him?"

"He's probably over at the Hansen House where he lives. It's two blocks east and one block north. It's a big white house."

"If you'll excuse me, miss, I'll see if I can find him."

Outside on the plank sidewalk, Will Jones looked back at the sign painted on the door. In big square letters it read, Maxwell Times. And in smaller, gothic letters was the message: "Nathan Benchley, Editor And Publisher."

Benchley. Now there's a name that has a literary ring to it, he thought. Too bad he couldn't take his mother's maiden name. Jones sounded like the name of an employee, not an editor and publisher.

Let's see, east two blocks and north one block. Why didn't she say turn left or turn right? East. Let's see. The street was alive with horse-drawn buggies, heavy freight wagons pulled by four-horse teams, and men on horseback. Pedestrians, men in jackboots and women in long skirts, clomp-clomped and tap-tapped on the plank walk. "Pardon me," he said, stepping aside to allow a severe-looking woman to pass.

Two of the streets were lined with square wooden buildings, some with two-story-high false fronts. A three-story building had a sign hanging over the walk which said it was the Wyatt Hotel, and the stone building at the end of the street had to be the new courthouse that Uncle Nathan had written about. Let's see, east. The sun was low in the sky over the courthouse. That had to be west. Will Jones turned east.

The Hansen House was easy to find. It was two-story Victorian, and it needed a fresh coat of white paint. But the dark blue shutters and the wide, bannistered porch were in excellent condition with each board and nail in place. He climbed the steps, crossed the porch and knocked lightly on the door. He waited a moment and knocked again.

The woman who opened the door was middle-aged and attractive in a plain sort of way. A little plump, but not too much. Bright blue eyes. "Yes sir?" She looked him over as though she were appraising him and liked what she saw.

"How do you do, ma'am," he said, lifting his hat. "My name is William C. Jones, and I was told I might find a Mr. Mahoney here."

"Jake Mahoney?"

"Yes, I believe that is his full name."

"He isn't here. Not right now. He'll be here by seven-thirty. That's when we serve supper. He never misses supper."

"Oh."

"Won't you come in, Mr. Jones?" She stepped back and smoothed down the white lacy apron over her billowy, ankle-length dress.

"That's very kind of you, ma'am, but I must locate Mr. Mahoney as soon as possible. You see, I'm trying to locate my uncle's—Mr. Benchley's—home. I understand he has—had—a house here in Maxwell."

A sudden understanding came over her face. "You're Mr. Benchley's nephew, aren't you. We heard that a nephew of his was coming from somewhere back East. Kansas City, isn't it? Well, we're mighty happy to have you here, Mr. Jones. We're sorry about your uncle. Mr. Benchley was a gentleman, and his accident shocked us all. If it's any comfort to you, he had a very nice funeral and a big headstone. You'll want to visit his grave, of course, and I'll be happy to tell you how to find it. It's real easy to find, and—"

He cut her off. "I just arrived on the stage from Leadville, madam, and I had to leave my luggage at the offices of the Divide Stage and Freight Company. I was told they close the office at seven o'clock, and I would like to find my uncle's house before then."

"Well, I can tell you how to get there. It's a small gray house just two blocks from here. You go north a block and turn west. It's in the middle of the block, and you'll recognize it because it's gray with white trim and real cedar shingles from Denver. There are some ponderosas in the front yard. It's a nice little

10

house. Have you got a key?"

"Yes, I have. It was sent in the mail shortly after the telegram arrived informing us of my uncle's death. An attorney named Justus DeWolfe mailed it to us. I must locate him, too, but that can wait until tomorrow."

"Would you care to take supper with us, Mr. Jones? We're having boiled brisket of beef and cabbage tonight. I generally don't serve meals to anyone but my boarders, but I'll make an exception in your case."

"Thank you very much. I appreciate your hospitality. But I must retrieve my luggage and get moved into my uncle's house. Would you be so kind as to inform Mr. Mahoney of my arrival? I must meet with him."

"I surely will. Jake, uh, Mr. Mahoney will be glad to hear that you're in town. He was afraid he'd have to move somewhere else to practice his trade. We hope you're planning to start up the newspaper again. Marybelle will be glad to hear about you too."

"Marybelle?"

"Yes. She and Jake did all the typesetting for Mr. Benchley. She was getting almost as fast at it as Jake."

"Oh yes. I, uh, I've met her. In the office."

"Oh really?" The woman's eyebrows went up. "I didn't know she was back. Her mother died, and she went to the reservation where her mother lived. She used to work here, waiting tables and cleaning rooms, and I offered her her job back. She said she'd work for me again if the newspaper stays shut down. She's a good worker."

"The reservation?"

"The Ute reservation. Her mother lived there, and her grandpa still does. Her dad died long ago. Mary-

11

belle is half Ute, you know."

"I see. Well, thank you very much, madam. I must be going."

"You're welcome, Mr. Jones. I'm Maggie Hansen, and if you don't want to cook for yourself or eat at the Iveywood Restaurant as Mr. Benchley did, I'll set another place at the table for you. We serve three hot meals a day except on Sundays and then we serve two meals. We have twelve boarders, two to a room, and we're always filled up, what with the mines and the smelter and everything."

"Thank you very much, Mrs. Hansen. I'll keep that in mind."

"We charge four dollars and fifty cents a week, or eighteen dollars a month, paid in advance. We wash the bed linens every week, and we keep the house clean."

"I'm sure you do, Mrs. Hansen."

"I miss Marybelle. She's a good worker, and she's neat and polite. Got an education, too. She can read and write as well as anybody around here. Went to Mr. Tucker's school, and she went to learn. Not like these rowdy kids. Mr. Tucker kind of took her under his wing and taught her to read books that most folks can't understand. Poor old Mr. Tucker finally had to retire. His eyesight is failing along with his general health. Has the consumption, you know. Came here from back East somewhere because he hoped this mountain air would heal his consumption, but it didn't, and he just keeps getting worse. Marybelle goes over to his house and reads to him sometimes. He surely enjoys her reading to him. He's a fine old gentleman."

"I must be going, Mrs. Hansen. I very much appreciate your help. Good evening." He replaced his hat, turned and went down the steps. He could feel her eyes on his back as he walked away. Nice lady. Talkative, but pleasant. Let's see, north a block and west. Hope the house is livable.

He found the house easily and had no trouble unlocking the door. When he went inside his breath caught in his throat, and shock caused his mouth to open and close wordlessly.

The room was a shambles.

A long sofa and two stuffed chairs had been turned over, the rug had been peeled back, and books had been opened and tossed aside.

Will Jones let out a long groan and muttered aloud, "Good God. What in hell's going on around here?"

Slowly, as if he couldn't believe what he was seeing, he walked through the house. In the room built for a bedroom but obviously used for a study, every drawer in a desk had been pulled out and the contents dumped on the floor. The bedroom was worse. The mattress had been pulled from the bed and turned over. Clothes had been yanked from hangers in an oak wardrobe and scattered about the room. The only rooms not touched were the water closet, with its long sheet-metal tub and washstand, and the kitchen with its wood-burning cook stove, wooden table, chairs, and cabinets.

He prowled through the house and wondered if anything valuable had been stolen. There was no jewelry, but he didn't know whether his uncle owned any. There was no money, but then his uncle would have kept his money in a bank. Well, he would have to locate the authorities and determine whether the destruction had been reported. Thieves, it seemed, were everywhere, even in a small frontier town high in the Colorado Rockies.

He was walking from the kitchen to the front door when a figure appeared in the doorway. Startled, he jumped back and glanced around for a weapon. Being from an eastern city, he carried no gun, and he saw nothing within reach that could be used for self-defense.

The figure in the door was almost as wide as it was tall, and at first glance it looked more like a bear or some other wild beast than a man. It spoke: "Mr. Jones?"

"Uh, uh, yes," he stammered, slightly shaken. Now he knew how the girl in the newspaper office felt.

"I'm Jake Mahoney. I'm told you wanted to see me."

Jones expected a guttural grunt or a growl out of the bear of a man, but its voice was only a little deeper than his own.

"Why, uh, yes, Mr. Mahoney. I do want to speak with you. Uh, Mr. Mahoney, do you have any idea what happened here?"

The figure came through the door and stopped in the center of the living room. It looked around, puzzled at what it saw. It had a square paper hat on its head, the kind that only printers knew how to fold out of newsprint, and it wore baggy jeans cut off at the ankles and held up by a tight belt.

"No. Looks like somebody was huntin' somethin', don't it? Prob'ly the same jaspers that busted into Mr. Benchley's desk over to *The Times*."

"Do you happen to know whether my uncle kept anything valuable in the house?"

"Nope. This's the first time I ever put foot in here. Did I get the rights of it? You're a kin of Nathan Benchley?"

"Yes. He was my uncle. Do you happen to know, Mr. Mahoney, whether this was reported to the authorities?"

"Don't b'lieve it was." He had a round face, smooth shaven, and a square jaw that looked like it was made of granite. "Least I never heard about it, and me and Marybelle hear about most things that happen around here." He wasn't very tall, about five foot eight, but he was incredibly wide across the shoulders, and the white buttons on his blue cotton shirt seemed about to pop off where the shirt was stretched across his broad chest.

"Well, it must be reported right away."

"Reckon it oughta. Don't surprise me none, howsomever."

"It doesn't?"

"No sir. Not after what happened to Mr. Benchley."

"What do you mean? He had an accident."

"That's what ever'body says, but me and Marybelle, we're guessin' somebody's dealin' off the bottom."

"Are you saying my uncle's death was not an accident?"

"Yup."

"Why? What else could it have been?"

"We're guessin there was some dirty dealin' there."

Jones studied the man closely, unbelieving. There

15

was no hint of a smile. The eyes, small, squinty, were dead serious. "Are you saying my uncle was murdered?"

"Yup. That's the rights of it."

Chapter Two

The telegram telling of Uncle Nathan's death had come on June 3, 1883, and it came at exactly the right time. Will Jones was restless, and he knew he was going to have to go somewhere and do something else, and he knew his mother wasn't going to like it. She was already disappointed in him. But after his father died, he just couldn't see her spending what little money she had on his higher education, and he had dropped out of Missouri U. after two years. He loved his mother dearly, but he couldn't stand to be dominated by anyone and he couldn't stand working in that dry goods store in Kansas City any longer.

He had to get away.

The telegram from Leadville, Colorado, didn't say anything except that Uncle Nathan had died and a letter with details would follow. His mother agreed, finally, that he would go to Colorado and determine whether the weekly newspaper established by Nathan was a worthwhile venture and whether he wanted to continue it. Though he kept it to himself, he had made up his mind before he left home. You bet your bottom dollar he wanted to continue it. If it was at all possible, he would take up where his uncle left off.

Mrs. Jones had persuaded him to wait for a letter from the lawyer, Justus DeWolfe. Jones couldn't possibly get to Maxwell, way out near Colorado's continental Divide, before Uncle Nathan's body had to be buried. Poor Mrs. Jones wept all day and all night over the death of her brother and wailed about how he wouldn't even have family at his funeral.

She wailed again when the letter arrived and told how Nathan Benchley had suffered before he died. The poor man received a compound fracture of the right leg when a horse fell on him in the mountains east of Maxwell, and there was no one around to help him. It was a wild and unpopulated country, the letter said, and it wasn't known how many days and nights had passed before one of Mr. Benchley's employees finally persuaded the county sheriff to organize a search party.

They found Uncle Nathan dead. The letter said he had died bravely, trying desperately to survive. Searchers found tracks which indicated that he had crawled and hopped on one foot for at least five miles before he became too exhausted to carry on. He had made a splint of tree limbs for his broken leg, but the fracture was so bad that a shard of bone had broken through the skin, and it was impossible for Mr. Benchley to put any weight at all on his right foot.

Poor Mrs. Jones cried all night again, thinking about how her brother had suffered. "Why," she wailed, "had Nathan gone out there to that godforsaken land where there was no one to help an injured man? Why had Nathan been so foolish?"

Jones knew why, but he couldn't explain it. It was

the same kind of restlessness he felt. Some men needed a challenge, adventure, something different. Uncle Nathan was that kind. Working in a dry goods store was no test of any man. Will wanted to be like his uncle.

But he didn't want Uncle Nathan to die.

"Mr. Mahoney," he said, uncertain of what he should say next, "we, uh, we need to talk about this, but I have to retrieve my luggage from the stage company offices and find a place to stay. This house isn't livable as it is. And we must inform the authorities of this."

"You can put up at the Wyatt Hotel. If you got more stuff than you can carry, I'll help."

"I'll have to stay at the hotel temporarily. I'll have to find someone to clean up this house and make it livable again."

"We'll find somebody. Uh, Mr. Jones, I'd like to ask . . . are you gonna put out a paper again?"

He had to consider his answer carefully. He had come to Maxwell determined to resume publication of *The Maxwell Times*. But though he had learned something about business management in college and working in a dry goods store, he knew nothing about the newspaper business. He didn't want to make a promise he couldn't keep.

Finally he said, "We'll see."

Why were there no books or ledgers showing how Uncle Nathan did business? Were they stolen? And why were there no back issues of the newspaper?

Jones had spent the night at the Wyatt Hotel and breakfasted at the Iveywood Restaurant, and now he was going through his uncle's desk in the office of *The Maxwell Times*.

"Where is everything?" he muttered to himself as he closed the bottom drawer in the old rolltop desk. "Every businessman keeps records of expenses, outlay, and income. There's got to be some ledgers somewhere."

He prowled through the long room, took a mental note of the roll of newsprint, the full cases of type, the flatbed press, and the keyboard typesetter. Everything seemed to be in order. He stood in the center of the room and looked down at the floor, trying to understand it all, and was startled again when he heard the clomp-clomp of heavy boots on the wooden floor. He sighed when he recognized the wide hulk of Jacob Mahoney.

"Mornin', boss," the printer said. "When we goin' to start shufflin' the deck?"

"Doing what?"

"Dealin' the cards, you know, settin' type.'"

"Well, we have to get a few things straightened out first. For instance, is this all the equipment my uncle had to print a newspaper?"

"Yup. It's enough, howsomever. For me and Marybelle. I can set four columns a day, and she can set three. And she can put type back in that outfit . . ." He nodded at the keyboard machine. "Faster than anybody you ever saw."

"How many pages has Uncle Nathan been printing?"

"Only four lately, but we usta put out six."

"Why fewer pages lately?"

"No ads. Usta get ten and sometimes twelve sticks of ads ever' week."

"Advertising, you mean?"

"Yup."

"Pardon my ignorance, Mr. Mahoney, but—"

"Call me Jake. Nobody calls me mister."

"Very well, if you wish. As I started to say, why did the advertising drop off."

"DamfIknow. Seems like Mr. Benchley ruffled somebody's feathers."

"The advertisers?"

"That's what I heered, but Mr. Benchley never talked business with me and Marybelle. He fired my other printer's devil when we run outa ads to set."

"Printer's devil?"

"My other helper. Like Marybelle, only Marybelle is a lot faster and smarter than he was."

"Um. I see. But the businessmen withdrew their advertising?"

"That's the skinny I get."

"Why are there no ledgers or back issues of the newspaper here?"

"They was stole. Least we think that's why somebody busted in here."

"Why?"

The husky printer pushed his folded paper hat back and squinted at the desk. "DamfIknow. Me and Marybelle, we can't cut their sign."

"Can't do what?"

"Can't figger it out."

"Where is Marybelle, uh, Miss Dubois now?"

21

"Prob'ly at Ben Tucker's. She took Mr. Benchley's death like a poke in the belly. She went back to the reservation when her old ma passed on and just got back day before yesterday. I hated to do it but I told her about Mr. Benchley, and she set down on that stool there and acted like the whole world was comin' down, what with her mother cashin' in and then Mr. Benchley. And when I told her about somebody bustin' in here and makin' a mess, she got mad and worried and scared, and we had a long palaver, and we figger there's some aces missin' in this whole deal."

"I'm sorry about her mother. Do you know where she's staying? I need to get together with the two of you sometime today."

"At old Ben Tucker's house. He usta teach school till his consumption got so bad he can't do nothin'. She usta go over and cook and clean up for him and read to him, but she's stayin' there now. He can't take care of hisself no more."

Jones crossed the room and sat in the spring-backed chair at his late uncle's desk. "I see."

"She'll show up."

Their conversation was interrupted by another figure in the door. This one was average height, but looked taller under his high-crown beaver hat. He wore a dark coat over a flowery vest with a gold watch chain draped across his stomach from one side vest pocket to another.

"Pardon me." He stepped onto the threshold and entered the room. His pants were creased down the front, and his black button shoes had pointed toes. "I've been told that you are Mr. William C. Jones, nephew of the late Nathan Benchley."

"Yes sir, I am." Jones stood, and the newcomer had to look up at his six-foot-three stature.

"Allow me to introduce myself." The man held out his hand, and Jones took it. "I am Wilbur Osgood, duly elected mayor of Maxwell. I want to extend a hearty welcome to you."

"That's very kind of you, Mr. Osgood."

"I also want you to know that we all were shocked and terribly saddened by the death of your uncle. He was a fine gentleman, and his passing was a blow to the community."

"Thank you, sir. My mother—his sister—is still in mourning. We were informed by mail that he had a decent burial."

"Oh, yes indeed. Though the funeral had to be arranged rather hastily, the whole town turned out, and the flags in Maxwell flew at half staff for a week. We had a casket made of pine and a tombstone chiseled from native granite."

"We very much appreciate that, my mother and I. We're sorry we were unable to attend, but it took three days on the train from Kansas City, and I had to wait for a stage in Leadville."

"We know. I don't mean to be insensitive, Mr. Jones, but you understand the body was deteriorating by the time we found him, and we have no undertaker here."

"Yes, of course. Won't you sit down, Mr. Osgood." He nodded at a wooden barrel-backed chair beside the desk. The printer, Jacob Mahoney, clomp-clomped his way to the back of the room, but stayed within hearing range.

Wilbur Osgood hitched up his long coat and sat in

23

the chair. He removed his hat and placed it on his right knee. "I didn't hear of your arrival until this morning. Only a few minutes ago as a matter of fact. I trust you spent a comfortable night in the hotel and had an acceptable breakfast."

"Yes, I did. The hotel has excellent accommodations, and my meal at the Iveywood Restaurant was well prepared."

"We have a table reserved at the restaurant, Mr. Jones, and you are most welcome to sit there."

"Excuse me, who has a table reserved?"

"Well, there's me, Sheriff Omar Schmitt, there's Oliver Scarbro who owns the mercantile, the banker Cyrus Dochstader, John Pope, owner of the Bijou smelter and mine, and, uh, a few other businessmen who also serve on the town council. We're building a new town hall. We've outgrown the one-room cabin that we have been using, and at times we meet informally at the restaurant. All public meetings are conducted in a public place, of course."

"I see."

"As editor and publisher of *The Times* you are welcome to join us, and you are welcome to take your meals at our reserved table. Uh, you are planning to resume publication, I expect?"

"I hope to, Mr. Mayor, but I haven't been able to locate my uncle's ledgers. You see, I know nothing about publishing a newspaper, and I need to look over his books and try to learn something of the business end."

"Oh, I'm sure Nathan kept books. They have to be in his desk here or in his home. He owned a very nice bungalow, you know. I suppose it will be your home

24

now."

"That's something else that puzzles me. My uncle's house has been ransacked. It looks as though someone was looking for something there."

"What?" Surprise showed on Wilber Osgood's face, and he straightened up in his chair. "The house was ransacked? Why in the name of . . . excuse me, Mr. Jones, but I'm shocked to hear of it. We have a clean town with very little crime and hooliganism. Does Sheriff Schmitt know of this?"

"Apparently not. Apparently no one knew of it until I entered the house yesterday evening. I have no idea when it happened."

"Well, I'll report this to the sheriff immediately. We will not tolerate that sort of activity in Maxwell."

"I don't know whether anything was stolen. Do you happen to know whether Uncle Nathan kept anything valuable in the house?"

"No, I'm afraid I do not. I, uh, have never been a guest in Nathan's home."

"I see. Well, I do want to meet with the authorities and report it. I would also like to know more details about my uncle's death."

"The details are, uh, gruesome, I'm afraid. You see, Nathan often rode horseback into the mountains and often stayed overnight. He liked to camp in the mountains. That's why no one became worried about him until several days after he left."

"Did it take long to find him?"

"Yes, it did. We had fifteen mounted men searching, but it took five days. You see, Mr. Jones, there's a terrible lot of territory up there, and no one had any idea where to begin a search. I'm afraid—again I apologize—I'm afraid the coyotes and magpies found him before we did."

"Magpies?"

"Yes. They are birds, carrion eaters."

"Oh." The picture that came to his mind caused his lips to tighten and a vile taste to form in his throat.

"I'm sorry to tell you this, Mr. Jones." The mayor of Maxwell stood. "I'll send Sheriff Schmitt over. Or the town marshal, Waller Vaughn. The sheriff must be in his offices at the courthouse now."

Jones swallowed a lump in his throat and got his voice back to normal. "I appreciate that, but please don't bother. I would like to see your courthouse anyway, and I'll go there."

"It's a beautiful courthouse. The general assembly was generous with us."

"The general assembly?"

"The state legislature in Denver."

"I see."

The mayor was right. The courthouse was beautiful. Built of moss rock, early American architecture, it had a red tile roof and marble columns bracing a wide front entrance. Inside, the floor was of polished marble, and the office doors were of hand-carved oak. His footsteps rang loudly on the floor as he looked for stairs going down to the bottom floor and the sheriff's office.

Sheriff Omar Schmitt was a portly man in his mid-forties, a man who obviously enjoyed eating. His jackboots were resting on an overturned wastebasket, and he leaned back in his desk chair as he observed the tall young man in gentleman's clothes enter his office.

"Sheriff Schmitt?"

"Yep."

"My name is William C. Jones. I'm the nephew of the late Nathan Benchley."

The jackboots came down from the wastebasket, and the sheriff sat up straighter. "Oh, you are." The words were spoken matter-of-factly. "I heard some kin was comin'." The sheriff stood and offered his hand. He was six feet tall and big in the shoulders as well as in the stomach. His sideburns came down to his jawline and widened there. He carried a pistol in a leather holster on his right hip. They shook briefly.

"I would like to learn more about my uncle's death, Mr. Schmitt, if you can spare a few minutes."

"Why shore. Old Benchley, uh, Mr. Benchley, was a personal friend. Have a seat there."

Jones sat in a wooden chair with a rounded back. "I've been told that Uncle Nathan often went up into the mountains alone, and I wonder, do you know why he did that?"

"Prospectin'. Ever'body around here does some prospectin' now and then. A lot of folks have got rich. The Bijou and her sister the Maggie are producin' some mighty rich ore. They're the richest gold mines anywhere. Gold and silver is our biggest industry."

"Prospecting? We, my mother and I, didn't know he was interested in searching for precious metals. He didn't mention that in his letters."

"Oh yeah. We've got gold, silver, lead, you name it and we've got it around here. It was gold that built this town. Ever'body gets hisself some diggin' tools

27

and goes up there now and then. Your uncle had a habit of takin' off right after the paper was out and he had time to spare. He rented two horses, a saddle horse and a packhorse, from the Ardmore Livery, and he sometimes stayed three-four days."

"How did he manage his business while he did that?"

"Weel, I don't know nothin' about managin' a business, but I do know old Jake and that breed girl worked just as hard when Nathan was gone as when he was there breathin' down their necks."

"The breed girl? Would that be the lady named Marybelle?"

"Yep. Purty. An educated Injun. Marybelle Doobwah, or somethin' like that. Old Tucker taught her to read and write."

"Doobwah? Is than an Indian name?"

"Naw. Her pappy was as white as you and me. I think he was a Frenchman, but I don't know for shore. Married a Ute squaw and had a daughter, then died of the consumption or pneumonia, or somethin'."

"Doobwah? Would that be spelled D-u-b-o-i-s?"

"Dunno. I never seen her name in writin', just heard it a couple of times."

"Uh, getting back to Uncle Nathan's death, I'm told it took five days to find his body after you started looking."

"Yep. There's a powerful lot of country up there, and nobody knew which way he went. Found his horses first. They was cinch sore, but fat from croppin' that mountain grass."

"Are you sure of what happened?"

"Positive. We backtracked and found where his horse turned over on him in some rocks and got up and left him afoot. The packhorse went, too. Left him with a busted leg and nothin' else."

"And he died in less than, let's see, it would be eight days?"

"Yep. He'd of been better off if he'd just stayed put and built hisself a fire. But he must a thought he could drag hisself out to a ranch road about ten miles north. Wore hisself out. Musta hurt like hell, that leg. Musta thought that road was closer than it was."

"I'm told he managed to travel approximately five miles with a compound fracture of the right leg."

"Just about. Didn't gain a thing. Been better if he'd stayed put."

"Did he have matches to build a fire?"

"Come to think of it . . ." The sheriff tilted his chair back and gazed at the ceiling. "Dunno. Got his stuff over here in the storeroom. Let's have a looksee."

He followed the sheriff's wide buttocks through a door into a small room piled with odds and ends, including digging tools, a bedroll, a saddle, pack saddle, canvas tents, cooking utensils, a broken chair, and a long-barreled rifle. "Let's see now." The sheriff grunted as he bent over and picked up a pair of dirty wool pants and a plaid shirt from the floor. "These are his clothes."

The sheriff went through the pockets, retrieved a folding knife, a handkerchief, some keys, and nothing else. "No matches. Had to of had some matches, though. Maybe in his panyers."

He picked up two canvas panniers with loops at the top, made to hang over the cross bucks of a pack

29

saddle, and turned them upside down. Cooking utensils, a slab of bacon, a loaf of bread, a butcher knife, canned food, a sack of sugar, and a sack of coffee fell out."

"Uh-huh," the sheriff grunted, picking up a box of wooden kitchen matches. "He had matches, but not in his pockets. Come to think of it he didn't smoke, I don't believe, and he prob'ly didn't carry matches in his pockets."

"So when his horses ran off, they left him without matches or anything."

"That's the way of it. Left him with a busted leg and nothin' else."

Chapter Three

Will Jones had another lump in his throat as he walked back toward the office of *The Maxwell Times*. It took Uncle Nathan five days and possibly longer to die. He had died in agony. Jones looked up at the purple mountains just east of the town and shuddered. What a wild and terrible place that must be. No one for miles and miles. Just wild animals. As the sheriff had said, it was lucky they found him at all. Men have been lost up there and never found.

Yet, it's kind of pretty, too. The mountains, covered with green coniferous trees and cathedral rocks, are beautiful when you forget about the isolation. He had traveled through them and over them on the Denver, South Park and Pacific train from Denver to the boom city of Leadville. It was the first time he had seen the mountains, and he found them extremely interesting.

When the steam engine finally made it to the top of the eleven thousand, five hundred-foot Boreas Pass, the conductor told him he was on the highest railroad in the world, and when they reached Leadville, elevation ten thousand, two hundred feet, he was told that that was the highest city in the nation. Will Jones was fascinated. Even when the railroad trestles swayed on their long spindly steel legs, and after the train went through the pitch-black mysterious Alpine Tunnel, he was wide-eyed at the wildness and beauty of the mountains.

But he shuddered again when his imagination pictured an injured man trying to find his way back to civilization, dragging a broken leg. The mountains were beautiful. But terrible, too.

Maxwell's main street was busy with wagons and buggies. Two heavily loaded ore wagons pulled by four-horse teams creaked past toward a mill on the east side of town. He guessed it was a mill of some kind because of the black smoke that erupted from a tall smokestack.

He walked past the Valley State Bank, spun around on his heels and went inside. A teller with a green eyeshade and garters on his sleeves looked him over carefully when he presented the cashier's check from the First National Bank of Kansas City. The teller excused himself politely and disappeared inside an inner office. When he came out he was followed by a well-dressed, well-groomed man who looked to be in his late fifties.

The man came around the long counter and offered his hand. "How do you do, Mr. Jones. I am Cyrus Dochstader, president and chairman of the board of this institution." Jones shook hands with him and again explained that he wasn't sure whether he would resume publication of *The Maxwell Times*, and listened again to condolences over the death of his uncle. He was assured he could write checks on his new account immediately.

32

Back at his uncle's desk in the newspaper office, he tried to decide what to do next and tried to understand what had happened. Murder? Not likely. Uncle Nathan had suffered a compound fracture of the right leg far from civilization and help, and he had died of exposure, dehydration, starvation, pain, and no telling what else. How could that be murder?

Yet Uncle Nathan's home had been ransacked, and his record books were missing. Too, there was that remark Jacob Mahoney had made. Advertising had fallen off, apparently because someone was angry with Uncle Nathan. Jones was no newspaperman, but he knew that advertising was a newspaper's prime source of revenue. That two cents per copy, or whatever the paper was sold for, wouldn't pay the bills.

Something strange was going on here, but Will Jones couldn't even begin to guess what.

For an hour or more he sat at his late uncle's desk, then decided that his next step should be a visit with the lawyer, Justus DeWolfe. He had to ask directions from a bearded man in rough working clothes on the street, but he had no trouble finding the three-room log cabin with the Attorney At Law sign on the door.

Justus DeWolfe sat at his desk, reading a law book. A long rack on the wall behind him was filled with books of Colorado statutes. A short, round young man, the lawyer stood and offered his hand when Jones introduced himself.

For the fourth time that morning, Jones listened to condolences, and again he said he wasn't sure about the future of *The Times*.

"First, I need to know more about my uncle's finances," he said. "His record books are missing."

"Missing?" The lawyer seemed astonished.

Jones explained it, then asked, "I was wondering whether I need a court order or anything to examine his bank records. I need to know whether I have the funds to carry on with the newspaper. The small amount I brought from home won't last long."

"We can easily look at his bank records. Your uncle gave me full power of attorney, and all we have to do is go over to the bank and ask."

"Power of attorney? Why did he do that?"

"I can only tell you what he told me, Mr. Jones, and that is he didn't want his property and funds tied up in probate if anything happened to him. He wanted you, his nephew, to be able to take over immediately."

"Strange." Will Jones looked at the collection of law books without seeing them. "He didn't mention anything like that in his letters to us."

"He signed the papers only a few days before he disappeared."

"Do you suppose he suspected something might happen to him?"

The lawyer shrugged. "He was close-mouthed, but yes, it's fair to suppose he did."

"Why?"

"As I said, Mr. Jones, your uncle kept everything close to his vest. I have no idea why. Unless it was because he often went into the mountains alone. Like a lot of people around here he had visions of striking it rich."

"Could his death have been murder?"

"Murder?" Justus DeWolfe's eyes widened in disbelief. "How could it have been? We have some experienced outdoorsmen around here, Mr. Jones, and the tracks and marks he left told the story just as plain as if it had been written on paper."

"Yeah." Jones was studying the floor now.

"Why do you suspect murder?"

"Oh, I really don't suspect it. It's just the things that have happened, his desk and his home rifled, his ledgers missing, giving you full power of attorney. I don't understand it. And, too, I've been told that advertising in *The Times* had fallen off to practically zero."

"That's true. Anyone could see that. He used to publish six pages a week, but lately it has been only four."

"I don't want to keep repeating myself, Mr. De-Wolfe, but why?"

The lawyer shook his head. "I don't know. What I do know is this town—that is, the people who run this town—are a very close-knit group. Nathan Benchley was one of the clique. I, uh, I came here only a few months ago, and I am not one of the privileged few."

"Um." Jones shook his head slowly, a worry frown between his eyes. Finally, he stood. "Well, whenever it's convenient, Mr. DeWolfe, I'd like to accompany you to the bank and look at the bank's records of my uncle's financial transactions."

The lawyer stood, too. "I can go now. I'll sign everything over to you." He pulled a watch out of his vest pocket, snapped the lid open and said, "Time for lunch. Would you care to have lunch with me before we go? They serve a tolerable meal at the Iveywood Restaurant. Of course, if you have other plans . . ."

"I have no other plans. I'd be happy to have lunch

35

with you."

The restaurant was crowded. Men of all descriptions sat at the counter and at the wooden tables covered with oilcloth. There were men in fancy vests and creased trousers and men in rough wool pants, baggy at the knees and seat, and men in denim overalls held up by suspenders.

A hand-painted sign on a wall behind the counter told everyone that roast beef or corned beef with mashed potatoes and boiled turnips was the meal of the day. Homemade peach pie was also available.

"Looks like we'll have to sit at the counter," said Justus DeWolfe. "Hope you don't mind." He led the way and parked his short round body on a vacant stool at the counter. Jones sat down on a stool next to him. A harried waitress in a long dress and long white apron took their order: two roast beef sandwiches and coffee.

"They keep their perishable foods in a shed out back that's filled with sawdust and ice cut from the pond last winter. Keeps it fresh for awhile, but not forever. Be careful what you eat."

Jones looked around and saw Mayor Wilbur Osgood come in with two other men. He recognized the banker Cyrus Dochstader, but not the other man. The mayor glanced his way and nodded.

"That's part of the clique," Justus DeWolfe said, following Jones's gaze. "They've got that table reserved."

Jones remembered that Wilbur Osgood had invited him to sit at their reserved table, but apparently the lawyer had not been invited.

When the sandwiches were served, Justus DeWolfe

picked his up, held it close to his nose, sniffed, and took a bite. Jones began eating without sniffing. It tasted good. When it came time to pay he was surprised at the price: thirty-six cents.

"They overcharge," the lawyer commented when they were out on the sidewalk, "but when you own the only decent restaurant in town you can charge anything you want. And some of the men around here have plenty of money. They don't care."

"This is the only restaurant in town?"

"No, there's another a couple of blocks south, but the men who inhabit the place aren't the kind I want to rub elbows with. I hear people have come down with ptomaine from the food."

"I guess they don't have an ice house, then."

"No. The only time they get any fresh meat is when they butcher it themselves. They buy beef, and they get a deer or an elk now and then."

On their way to the bank they walked past the Totten House of Spirits, with its stained glass windows and heavy oak doors. "Are you a drinking man, Mr. Jones?"

"Oh, I imbibe occasionally. I don't have the habit, however."

"Same here. That's the only decent place to drink. There's another saloon, called the Deerfoot, two blocks south, next door to the Ace Cafe, but your life isn't worth much in there."

"Is there a marshal or anyone besides the sheriff to keep the peace?"

"Oh yes. Marshal Waller Vaughn has been known to bend his gun barrel over a few heads, and he took a shotgun and threatened to send another troublemaker to his grave a couple of months ago. He's as tough as any of them, and he won't take any sass. He was keeping his arrestees in an old log jail, but they busted out as fast as he could lock them in. Now that they've built a new jail in the basement of the courthouse, no one breaks out."

Will Jones was disappointed when he saw his late uncle's bank balance: two hundred and thirty dollars. He had no idea how much it cost to publish a newspaper, but he knew it cost something, and apparently *The Times* had not shown a profit for several months. Some of the checks written by his uncle were for newsprint and ink. Wages for the employees was another expense. Jacob Mahoney was paid one dollar and seventy-five cents per day. Marybelle Dubois was paid one dollar and ten cents per day. Another check stub showed a payment to the American Press Service in Denver.

No checks had been made out to the employees for over a month. Jones wondered how they had been living. Well, he would either have to advise them to look for employment elsewhere or pay them and put them to work.

Chapter Four

Outside the bank, Jones and Justus DeWolfe shook hands and parted. Jones walked back to the newspaper office with his head down, trying to decide what to do. He bumped shoulders with a bearded man in a floppy hat, saying, "Pardon me, sir," and stepped off the plank walk into the street.

A one-horse buggy would have run over him had not the horse shied and swerved away from him. The driver hauled on the lines to get the horse trotting straight ahead and looked back at Jones with a menacing glare.

Two young ladies in long skirts and lacy hats looked up at his six-foot-three frame and tittered coquettishly. He paid them no mind.

A shrill steam whistle split the air, and he looked up at the mill on the east side of town, guessing the whistle was a signal for the employees to return to work after their noon hour.

He reminded himself to square his shoulders as he walked, something he was always trying to remember to do.

The door to the newspaper office was locked, and

he couldn't remember whether he had locked it. He fished the long, flat key out of his pocket, inserted it in the keyhole and stepped onto the threshold. Leaving the door open, he sat at his uncle's desk, unmindful of the black flies that flew inside, buzzed around his head and flew around the room.

For a moment he sat there, then got up and walked around, looking at the press and equipment. There was a roll of newsprint, but he had no idea how many pages it amounted to. There was ink in the well beside the inking rollers, but he had no idea how long it would last. The type cases were full. Apparently what was needed to put out a few newspapers was there, but he had no idea how many the equipment could print.

And when he thought about it, what would they print? What would they do for news? He could write. His English composition teacher at Missouri U. wouldn't have passed him on to his junior year if he hadn't learned to write well. But what would he write?

He stood in the center of the room with his hands shoved deep into his pockets and let his shoulders slump as he worried about it. If he had some of the newspaper's back issues he could study them and get an idea of what Uncle Nathan did, what he wrote and where he got his news.

"Oh boy," he said to himself, "I've got to do something and I don't know what to do. Let's see, there just has to be some back issues somewhere. Someone has to have kept some old newspapers for some reason or other."

He locked the door behind him and headed for the Hansen House. Mrs. Hansen semed to be a sociable sort. Maybe she would have some back issues. Or was it Miss Hansen?

She opened the door soon after he knocked and seemed happy to see him. "Why, Mr. Jones. Won't you come in." She stood back and allowed him to enter. He removed his hat as he stepped into a foyer with a wide staircase at the opposite end and doors opening into other rooms. A braided rug covered a small part of the oak floor. Maggie Hansen had her brown hair pulled back loosely and tied in a bun at the back of her head. A handsome woman, he thought again. She was smiling a nice smile.

"I'm so happy to see you, and we're all happy that you are planning to put out a paper again. We all miss *The Times*."

"Well, I'm not sure, Mrs. Hansen—excuse me, is it Mrs. or Miss Hansen?"

"Mrs. My husband died last winter. He owned the Maggie Mine."

"I'm sorry. About the paper, I need some time to make a decision. I was wondering, Mrs. Hansen, whether you by any chance happen to have some back issues of *The Times*. You see, someone broke into the office and took my uncle's record books and all the printed papers."

"Oh yes, I heard. Why would anybody want to do that?"

"I haven't a clue. Anyway, I thought I might learn something from some back issues if I can find any."

"I'll look. Won't you be seated."

He sat on a padded bench under a tall mirror while she rummaged through a stack of pulp magazines and letters on a table across the vestibule from him.

"There's none here," she said. "Let me look in the kitchen."

It was quiet in the house while she was gone, and he wondered why, then guessed that her boarders were all working men who were at work. In a few minutes she was back, carrying some newspapers.

"I found two, Mr. Jones. In the kitchen. We use old newspapers to start a fire in the cook stove every morning, and I found these in the kindling box."

Standing, he remembered to straighten his shoulders. "Thank you very much. I appreciate this."

"Have you visited Mr. Benchley's grave yet? You'll be pleased when you do. He had a fine funeral, nearly everybody went. Reverend Bennett delivered a fine eulogy, and there were lots of flowers that people gathered from the mountains. Have you decided where you're going to take your meals? Like I said yesterday you're more than welcome to eat here, and my other boarders would be honored to share the table with the editor and publisher of *The Times*."

"No, I haven't been to the cemetery yet. In fact, I haven't decided anything yet. I'm sure your boarders are charming, or, uh, fine gentlemen."

"Marybelle used to stay here even after she started working for the newspaper, but now she's staying with Mr. Turner and taking care of him, except on Sundays, when she always disappears and nobody knows where she goes."

"Miss Dubois? She disappears?"

"Oh yes, she always leaves after dark on Saturdays and comes back after dark on Sundays. When anybody asks where she goes she just smiles and says nothing."

42

"Well, I must be going. You see, I'm just sort of groping my way around now, Mrs. Hansen. Thanks very much for the papers." He didn't put his hat on again until he was out the door and off the porch.

The cemetery would have to wait. As his dad had said once when an aunt died, "The time to do things for people is when they're alive, not after they're dead." What couldn't wait was the newspapers Jones carried. He just had to get back to the office and read them.

Well, Jones thought after he'd read through the papers and tilted his chair back, it was interesting. At least he knew now where to look for news. The sheriff and the town marshal had been the source of news about crime, the mayor had been quoted on what was happening in the local government, likewise the chairman of the Maxwell County Board of Commissioners. Some cattle were stolen from a ranch called the Double B Bar, owned by a Max Pendergast, and a hog was stolen from a pen on the south side of town. The mayor was quoted as saying the city of Maxwell was financially solvent, thanks to the mines and the smelter.

Then there was a story about a new vein of silver being found in a canyon about five miles east and a claim being filed by a Josef Grunenwald, who boasted that it was a rich vein.

Another issue quoted Sheriff Schmitt as saying the cattle were stolen at least a month earlier, and Rancher Pendergast estimated that about fifty head were missing. The sheriff guessed they were being driven northeast, and he vowed to alert authorities in the South Park country to watch for them.

Jones wondered how fifty head of cattle could be missing for a month before anyone knew they were gone, but then he remembered reading about how unbelievably large some of the cattle ranches were out West.

Everything in the papers appeared to be good news economically. More precious minerals were being discovered, the two largest mines, the Bijou and the Maggie, were producing high-grade ore, and the Bijou Smelter and Reduction Works was going full blast. The owner, John Pope, was planning to build another furnace in the near future. There was also some news about a sawmill on the north edge of town, and the owner was quoted as saying he was planning to add another blade.

Then why, Jones wondered, was there no advertising in the newspapers? What had Uncle Nathan done to make the advertisers mad at him?

The last issue was dated May 24, 1883, the day Uncle Nathan was last seen. One full column on the front page consisted of an editorial written by the editor and publisher.

It said nothing of interest, but after reading it Jones decided he would have to write a front page editorial for the next edition. It seemed to be expected of the editor and publisher.

There was some national news and news from the state capital, Denver, which, Jones guessed, came by mail from the American Press Service in Denver. A dispatch from Washington read: "Secretary Teller, Secretary Lincoln, General Crook, and Mr. Price,

Commissioner of Indian Affairs, conducted a conference in the War Department in regard to the disposition of captured Apache Indians . . ."

When the printer Jacob Mahoney came in, Jones sat up straighter and squared his shoulders. Behind the printer came the girl Marybelle Dubois. Mahoney was carrying that big pistol in a holster fastened to his belt.

"Afternoon, boss," Mahoney said. "I hear you found some back issues."

"Why yes. Mrs. Hansen was kind enough to find some for me."

"Well, we got your house fixed up. Me and Marybelle, we mucked 'er out and fixed 'er up. Marybelle, she washed the bed sheets and hung up your uncle's clothes."

"You did?"

"Yep. It's fit to live in again."

"But why?"

The girl had been hanging back, letting the printer do the talking, but now she spoke. "We want you to be comfortable, Mr. Jones, in hopes that you will resume publication." She had a nice voice, not what he expected a half-breed Indian to sound like.

"Well, I certainly do thank you. This kind of reception is something I didn't expect."

"Fixed the lock on the back door. It was busted. Nobody can bust 'er now."

"Let me pay you for your labor." He reached for his new checkbook in his coat pocket. "And I meant to ask, did my uncle owe you any wages before he disappeared?"

"No," the girl said. "He paid us up to date when

the last paper came off the press. And thank you, but we didn't expect to be paid for cleaning your house."

"Naw. You don't owe us nothin'. We're only hopin', Marybelle and me, that we'll have a job here again."

"If it's at all feasible, you will have, but at the moment I can make no promises. Tell me, did my uncle do all the writing for the newspaper?"

"Yes sir," the girl said. "He . . ." She looked away. "He didn't trust anyone else to write in a journalistic style."

Jones read discouragement in her voice and took another, longer look at her. She was of average height, slender, with those high cheekbones common among Indians—at least the Indians he had seen in pictures—and those wide-spaced brown eyes. Her color was dark, well, not very dark; more like a dark suntan, perhaps. What was it the sheriff said about her? "Purty." Well, that's what she was, with her straight nose, firm mouth and chin, and long graceful neck. Her dark hair was almost straight, but had a slight bow over her ears. The French blood, probably. He guessed her age at about twenty-five.

She was embarrassed at the way he was looking at her, and she half turned, facing Mahoney.

"I, uh . . ." Jones wished he could say something to make her smile. "I'm not so sure I can write in a journalistic style either." When that brought no response, he added, "It's been some time since you've received a paycheck. Can I advance you some cash? Do you need living expenses?"

That brought a grin from Mahoney. "Now that's right thoughtful of you, boss, and I have to admit, Mrs. Hansen is after me to pay my board."

"Well then." Jones began to write in his checkbook. "This will help carry you over." He tore out the check and handed it to him. "You can cash it immediately at the Valley State Bank. I just opened an account there. Now." He looked at the girl. "How about you, Miss Dubois? Do you need an advance?"

"Thank you, but no, I have been living in the home of Mr. Tucker, a retired schoolteacher."

"I see. Well." Jones looked around the room for another chair, got up and carried a stool from near the press and set it down beside the barrel chair next to his desk. "We need to talk. Won't you both be seated?"

They sat, Mahoney in the barrel chair and the girl on the stool. Mahoney slouched, but the girl sat up straight with her feet together on the floor and her hands in her lap.

"I must admit," Jones began, a frown between his eyes, "that I know absolutely nothing about publishing a newspaper, and it has occurred to me that I will have to depend on you two for help and advice."

They listened, their faces expressionless.

"Can you tell me: Do we have everything it takes to publish a newspaper? I mean equipment, materials, and everything?"

They glanced at each other, then the girl spoke. "We have enough newsprint to print one thousand copies of four pages each week for the next four weeks, Mr. Jones. We have enough ink to last about five weeks. If we print six pages, we will run out of paper and ink in three weeks."

"Um. Is that what my uncle has been printing? One thousand copies?"

"Yes sir."

"Can you tell me where he gets—got—paper and ink?"

"I'm sorry, sir. He did all the ordering himself, and I don't know. Perhaps you can find the name of the companies from his bank records." It was obvious that she was choosing her words carefully.

"Um, yes, of course."

"I do know, sir, that it takes at least three weeks to get the materials from Denver. I have heard him worry out loud about how long it takes, and he did mention that it has to come from Denver via the Denver, South Park and Pacific Railroad and from Leadville by wagon."

"Um." He stared at her, somewhat amazed. She sat primly and stared back at him.

"You're very helpful, Miss Dubois. What you're saying is that if we're to publish a newspaper, I had better get going and order more paper and ink. Tell me, how much does—did—my uncle order at time?"

"I never saw one of his written orders, sir, but when it was delivered there were two rolls of newsprint weighing about two hundred pounds each and four thirty gallon drums of ink."

What was becoming evident here, Jones realized, was that Uncle Nathan considered his employees nothing more than laborers who weren't supposed to know anything about business management. But this young lady was smarter than Uncle Nathan had guessed.

He stared at her again. The more he looked at her the prettier she became. He wished she would smile.

"Miss Dubois, what is the fastest way to order

materials from Denver?"

"The stage drivers have been dependable about taking messages to the telegraph office in Leadville, sir. And they have been dependable about delivering telegrams back here. They're faster than the United States mail."

"So, the first thing I have to do is learn the name of the company in Denver, then write a telegram and leave it at the stage and freight company offices?"

"Yes sir."

"Well then." He stood. "I'd better get over to the bank again."

They stood, too. The printer had been quiet, but now he said, "Does this mean that you, uh . . ."

"I'll make a decision tomorrow." Jones answered. "That's a promise."

The girl's face changed expressions slightly, and for a second there he thought she might smile.

Chapter Five

While he walked to the bank, Will Jones tried to do some mathematics in his mind. Let's see, Uncle Nathan was paying about seventeen dollars and ten cents per week for labor, and his other expenses had to have been at least that much, and that would put his weekly expenses at—let's say thirty-five dollars. It cost thirty-five dollars to print four pages a week, and if he printed only one thousand papers which he sold at two cents each, his revenue was only twenty dollars per week. Without advertising revenue he was losing fifteen dollars a week. Maybe more.

Jones stopped and looked down at the plank walk. It would be foolish to order more supplies now. The thing to do was to meet with the merchants and see if he could drum up some advertising. If he could, fine. If not, it would be foolish to resume publication of *The Times*.

A miner with a ragged derby hat bumped into him as he stood in the middle of the sidewalk. "Pardon me," Jones said. The miner said, "Shore," spat a brown stream of tobacco juice into the street and went on his way.

What to do? How to meet with the advertisers? Just walk into their stores and introduce himself?

Mayor Wilbur Osgood had invited him to sit at a table reserved for the town fathers. Maybe that was the best place to meet them.

Jones crossed the street, having to wait until a freight wagon passed and having to run four steps to cross ahead of a buggy, and turned toward the court-house. He remembered seeing a small frame building near the courthouse with a sign out front that read, City Hall.

Mayor Osgood wasn't in at the moment, a woman with a slender figure but bad teeth had told him. Would he care to wait a few minutes? The mayor should be back momentarily. Yes, he would wait, Jones said, settling his tall frame into an unpadded wooden chair by the woman's desk. There was one other desk in the room, and there was obviously only one room.

He waited a half hour and looked at his watch. It was nearing six o'clock. "Are you sure the mayor will be back?" he asked.

"He said he would be back before I go home," she answered.

At six o'clock, Mayor Wilbur Osgood bustled in the door, removed his tall hat and shook hands again with Will Jones. "I don't remember whether I mentioned it this morning, Mr. Jones, but we are building a new city hall. It should be completed in another six weeks, then I will have a place to meet privately. Until then . . ." He shrugged, sat at his desk and swiveled his chair around to face Jones.

The tall young man with the thick brown mous-tache explained what he wanted and the mayor was agreeable. "I'll set up a meeting as soon as possible,"

51

he promised.

"Could it possibly be tonight, Mr. Mayor? You see, I have to make a decision about whether to resume publication, and the sooner the better."

"Yes, I think that can be arranged. Say seven-thirty?"

"I'm indebted to you, sir." Will Jones unfolded his tall body, remembered to straighten his shoulders and stuck out his hand.

He decided to move out of the hotel. If the paper was losing money, he couldn't afford to stay in the hotel. His uncle had lived alone in a nice little bungalow, and he could, too. It took two trips to carry his three valises to the small gray house with white trim, but he made it with time to spare. The house was spotless, and everything was in place. The bed was made and the sheets and blankets were clean. His uncle's alarm clock sat, wound and ticking, on a nightstand next to the bed, and his uncle's razor strop, razor, shaving mug, soap, and towels were laid out in the water closet.

Will Jones made a necessary visit to the little house out back, and there found another copy of *The Maxwell Times*.

This was an older issue, and it contained advertising. There was an ad from the Valley Mercantile about some bargains in silks and dress goods, and one lot of ginghams, fast colors. There was an ad from the Iveywood Restaurant and Josef Grunenwald. Jones counted what amounted to two full pages of advertisements. Plus, there was another column of legal notices from the Maxwell County clerk.

The national news was dull. The state news was anything but. A dispatch with a Denver dateline read:

"At two o'clock this morning Governor Grant received the following telegram from Hot Sulphur Springs: 'Commissioners and the county clerk of Grand County were all shot this afternoon by a masked mob. We, the undersigned citizens, request and pray that the Honorable Governor send at once a company of militia for the protection of its citizens.'"

Good God, Jones said to himself. He read on and learned that the Grand County commissioners were in the middle of a controversy about a proposal to move the county seat from Hot Sulphur Springs to Grand Lake. One of the masked men was also shot, and when the mask was removed he was identified as an opposing commissioner.

Jones couldn't believe it. Civilized men killing each other over a political dispute. But he had heard—and read—that the frontier West wasn't as civilized as the eastern cities. The next dispatch he read left no doubt about that.

It was datelined Maysville, Colorado, and it told about a group of masked vigilantes breaking into a jail and hanging two men accused of robbery and murder.

Shaking his head sadly, Jones wondered how long it would take civilization to reach the frontier. A responsible newspaper could help. He pondered that, and finally read the advertisements again. Of course, he said to himself, a newspaper could help, but you have to have advertising revenue to put out a paper.

He got to the Iveywood Restaurant at exactly seven-thirty and found Sheriff Schmitt and five well-dressed men already seated at the reserved table. Mayor Osgood beckoned him over and introduced him all around.

There were Oliver Scarbro, owner of the Valley Mercantile, John Pope, owner of the Bijou and Maggie Mines and the Bijou Smelter and Reduction Works, Josef Grunenwald, restaurateur and owner of Drugs and Sundries, and the banker Cyrus Dochstader. "We expect to be joined momentarily by Thom Douglas, who owns the harness and leather goods store," the mayor said. Douglas arrived just before dinner was served, and somehow he gave Jones the impression that he felt out of place there.

It was the same roast beef that Jones had had for lunch, only now it was covered with brown gravy and served with boiled potatoes and canned corn. Mayor Osgood waited until dinner was over and coffee was served before he lit a thick black cigar and got down to business.

"Gentlemen," he said, "I want to say at the outset that I personally am happy to have with us such an intelligent and personable young man as the new editor and publisher of *The Maxwell Times*."

"Hear, hear," someone said. Everyone except Jones and Thom Douglas had cigars going by now, and the air around the table was heavy with smoke.

"Can we take it, then, that you are going to resume publication?" asked Douglas.

"Well." Jones was uncertain of just how to answer that. He decided to be frank. "It depends a great deal on what transpires here tonight."

No one spoke. All eyes were on him, waiting for him

54

to continue.

"We're all businessmen here, and I don't have to tell you that without your advertising the newspaper lost money. I don't have all the figures available, but it is clear that my uncle, Nathan Benchley, was rapidly running out of funds. A newspaper needs—must have—the support of the community. Now, I don't know what the population of Maxwell is . . ."

"About two thousand," Douglas offered, "and there's that many more people living in the placer camps to the east and north."

"I'm told," Jones continued, "that my uncle printed one thousand copies a week, and sold them for two cents each. That doesn't begin to pay the bills. If we hustled, we could probably sell more newspapers than that, but our costs would increase as rapidly as our income. It seems to me—and I don't profess to know anything about your business or the market in this area—but it seems to me that advertising in the newspaper would increase your sales and net you far more than the cost of advertising."

They remained quiet, waiting to see whether he had more to say. He glanced at their faces. They were watching him. "Suppose, just suppose we increased our circulation and reached the mining camps that are closer to Maxwell than to Leadville. If we did that, and you advertised your goods and services in our paper, well . . ." He spread his hands and let them figure it out in their own minds.

Oliver Scarbo began nodding his head. "We might . . . people in the camps who have been going to Leadville to buy supplies and such might, just might be persuaded to come here. We're closer."

"Exactly," said Jones.

"Let me ask you, Mr. Jones," the restaurateur said, "when do you expect to increase your circulation and how do you propose to deliver newspapers to the mining camps?"

Again he had to be careful with his answer. He took a sip of coffee and wiped his mouth with a linen napkin. "Gentlemen, I must confess I know nothing about publishing a newspaper, but I do know that with your, uh, cooperation, I will order more materials first thing in the morning, and start setting type and do whatever it takes to get a paper out right away. As for increasing production, that will depend on costs and equipment, but I promise you that I will do that as soon as it is economically feasible."

"Suppose, just suppose, that we spend money advertising in your newspapers." Oliver Scarbro spoke slowly, thoughtfully. "Can we depend on you to . . . well, let me put it this way. If we cooperate with you, will you cooperate with us?"

He answered immediately. "I need your cooperation, and I will do everything in my power to see that your businesses prosper."

"Hear, hear," said Mayor Osgood.

He was bone weary when he went back to his uncle's house late that night, so weary that his legs ached with fatigue. His mind was whirling around in his head, spinning figures until they all massed together in one shapeless lump. He was worried, and after he crawled into his uncle's bed, he lay awake for hours.

The alarm clock on the nightstand ticked mercilessly until he got out of bed, took it into the water closet and closed the door. Could it be done? As things stood, the profit margin would be very small, maybe nonexistent. Could he increase production? How? Good God, he didn't even know what newsprint and ink cost. It would take more money than Uncle Nathan had in his checking account, and he would have to gamble some of his mother's money. She couldn't afford to lose it. If he failed, had to give up and leave town broke, he would never forgive himself. What would he do then? Go back to the dry goods store in Kansas City? Yeah, that's what he'd have to do. He'd have to earn a living for his mother.

What to do?

When he was able to look out the bedroom window at the break of dawn and see the vague shape of one of the ponderosas in front of the house, he got out of bed, lit two oil lamps, shaved and dressed. By daylight he was at the Iveywood Restaurant, but found it closed. A sign on the door said it would open for breakfast at six o'clock.

He remembered hearing about another cafe, the Ace, two blocks south, and he went looking for it. Inside, he sat at a counter made of rough lumber and read a handwritten menu on the wall. Other customers looked at him curiously, but were too busy eating and preparing for the early morning shift at the mill to comment on his fine clothes, unlined face, and smooth hands.

The waiter wore a once-white apron around his middle. It was smeared with some kind of cooking grease. "Yeah?" Jones politely ordered three hotcakes, bacon, and coffee.

When it was served, he dug into it with a bent fork and was surprised to find it tasty. He asked the man in working clothes next to him to please pass the syrup, and the syrup pitcher was shoved toward him. The man didn't look up.

"Thank you."

The man, with a week's growth of black whiskers, looked at him then, curiously, but said nothing and soon went back to shoveling food into his mouth.

Jones wondered whether he should smell the bacon before eating it, and decided that that would be too unmannerly, and ate it anyway.

It was six-fifteen by his watch when he plopped down wearily at his late uncle's desk. He found some blank newsprint that had been cut into letter-sized sheets, and with a lead pencil began doing some adding, subtracting, and dividing.

At six-thirty Jacob Mahoney came in followed by Marybelle Dubois. They said, "Good Morning," and stood in front of him, their faces blank.

Will Jones turned his back to them, tapped the desktop with the end of his pencil and frowned at the figures. Finally, he swiveled around to face them.

"Yes."

Their faces instantly came alive. The girl smiled a wide-open smile, and her teeth gleamed against her dark skin. Mahoney grinned from ear to ear.

"Yes, by George, we're going to put out a newspaper."

Chapter Six

Jacob Mahoney started rolling up his sleeves. "Let's get started. What's first, boss?"

"Well." Jones grinned at their enthusiasm. "First we have to have something to print. I met with some of the merchants last night, and I've got some commitments from them. I'll start gathering their ads as soon as the stores open for business. Then, while you're setting that in type, I'll make the rounds and gather and write some news. I think I know how to do that after reading what Uncle Nathan wrote."

"Can I help?" the girl asked. "With gathering and writing news, I mean."

"Well, no." He looked down and ran a hand over the top of his head. "I think Jake will need your help setting type."

"Oh." She was disappointed. But then she smiled again. "We'll be eagerly awaiting the first ad."

By ten o'clock Jones had enough ads to fill two pages, and he went next to the Maxwell County clerk's office at the courthouse to pick up some legal notices. They were to be set in six-point type, he was told. Jones didn't know what that meant, but he was sure Jake Mahoney would know.

His two employees looked at the sheets of paper the ads were scrawled on and nodded their heads with satisfaction. "That there'll go twenty-four points," Mahoney said, putting his finger on the top line of an advertisement for the Valley Mercantile. "This six-point stuff is the hardest. We have to set that a piece at a time."

"I'll do that," the girl said, taking the paper with legal notices back to the cases of type.

"This one goes front page, two columns," said Mahoney, studying a sheet from the Valley Mercantile. At the top of the sheet were the words: "The Following Great Inducements." Below that was the message: "Are Being Offered To All Citizens of Maxwell County." And below that was a list of bargains, including Hostetter's Stomach Bitters.

"The head'll go eighteen points and the subheads twelve," Mahoney said. "We can set the rest in eight-point and get 'er all in two columns. How about that, boss? We got nothin' but Bodoni Bold, but I guess they know that."

All Will Jones could do was shake his head and agree weakly, saying, "Whatever you say."

He stood there with his hands in his pockets, watching his employees work. They were happy, and Mahoney was whistling quietly through his teeth. The girl was taking type out of a case, a single letter, then a complete word, then a single letter, and setting it in a sheet-metal tray, which Jones guessed, consisted of a newspaper column.

Mahoney stood at the keyboard and punched keys one at a time. Each time he punched a key with the end of a forefinger it released a piece of type from a magazine and dropped it into a narrow tin column. After a while he gathered the pieces of type from the column in one big hand, carried them to the flatbed "chase," and separated them into words and lines. In his hip pocket was a short flat pica rule he used to measure the type, and on a leather thong dangling from his belt was a quoin, a tool for tightening the chase.

"How long will it take," Jones asked, "to do all this?"

"A couple of days," Mahoney answered, then resumed his whistling.

"I see. Then if we have four pages of news that would take another three days."

"Yep. Five days to set the type and another day to run the press," Mahoney said. "We can do 'er in less time if you want."

"How many hours a day do you work?"

"Around twelve, but we can put in more time if you need us, can't we, Marybelle."

"Yes sir." She didn't look up from her work.

"Well, I'll be darned," Will Jones said, shoving his hands deeper into his pockets. "I'll just be darned."

Sheriff Omar Schmitt was the first source of news. A timberjack was in jail waiting sentencing for shooting a mill workman in a brawl at the Deerfoot saloon. The mill employee was taken to Leadville and was still hospitalized. Jones learned that Maxwell County had

61

no full-time judge, and a judge came over from Leadville on Mondays to handle whatever litigation there was to handle.

He also learned that the state was planning to provide a full-time judge for Maxwell when the population of the county reached six thousand. The only municipal judge was the mayor himself.

They had never had a trial, and Jones was told that nobody was arrested unless he was caught with the stolen goods, or there were witnesses to a crime of violence. Then the arrestee pleaded guilty and was jailed. The Maxwell County jail now housed three prisoners.

All this was news, and Jones took notes until his fingers ached.

Next he went to the mayor's office, found he wasn't in, and went back to the county clerk. There, he learned that the county board of commissioners met once each month, and the next meeting was planned for three weeks in the future.

Jones learned that three more mining claims had been filed since the last issue of *The Times* had gone to press, and he wrote down the information.

Back at the mayor's office, Mayor Wilbur Osgood showed him a handwritten note from a resident of Leadville who hoped to open a saloon on Coulter Street, which, he found out, was the same street the Deerfoot saloon and the Ace Cafe were on.

After another roast beef sandwich at the Iveywood, Jones went back to his uncle's desk—his desk now—and began to write. He had no training or experience in journalism, but he studied his late uncle's style of writing and tried to copy it. The sentences were all long, with at least one clause in each, and the paragraphs were long.

Slowly, painstakingly, Jones wrote.

At seven o'clock he dotted the last sentence on a story about a full-time judge planned for Maxwell, looked at his watch, stood and stretched. His two employees were still working.

"Hey," he said, flexing his fingers to get the cramps out, "it's supper time. Mrs. Hansen told me she serves at seven-thirty. You don't want to miss supper, do you?"

Jacob Mahoney was bending over the flatbed chase. He straightened and looked at his own pocket watch. "By George, it is," he said. "I got to go. I'll come back after supper if you want, boss."

"Oh no. That won't be necessary at all. You've both earned your day's pay. Miss Dubois, where do you take supper? Do you eat at the Hansen House, too?"

"No sir." She pushed a strand of dark hair away from her eyes. "I'll cook supper for Mr. Tucker. He's not able to get around much." Her fingers were ink stained, and she had a smudge of ink on her right cheek.

"Whatever. I'll lock the door behind you. No need to come back tonight."

His own supper was hardly a full meal, but Will Jones was too weary to do anything more than empty a can of beef hash and a can of beans in a skillet, heat it on top of the wood-burning stove in his uncle's house and eat out of the skillet. He wished he had some fresh milk and wondered where he could buy some.

After supper he pumped a pail of water out of the short-handled pump at the steel sink, heated it on the stove, poured it into the long tin bathtub in the water closet and washed himself. That done, he put on his nightshirt and got into bed. He was pleased with the day. He had enough advertising to pay expenses and maybe leave a little profit. The business community seemed happy to have him there and seemed eager to cooperate. In fact, he could see no reason why *The Maxwell Times* couldn't turn out to be a profitable venture.

Of course there was that nagging thought at the back of his mind—that question of why the advertising had suddenly dropped off before Uncle Nathan died. But he was too weary to think about that now, and he let his mind and body relax. While the night wind sighed through the ponderosas outside his bedroom window, Will Jones slept.

It was the printer Jacob Mahoney who brought news next morning. He was already at work when Jones found the door to *The Maxwell Times* unlocked and stepped onto the threshold. Mahoney hurried toward him, his wide figure looking like an approaching freight train.

"Boss, I heered it whilst we was feedin' our maps. They found the Cuddigan boy dead, and they think he was beat to death."

"Who? What?" That was all Jones could say at the moment.

"The Cuddigan boy, the kid from the orphanage over to Leadville."

64

Jones sat down in the desk chair and smoothed down his brown moustache. "Who is . . . what happened?"

"The Cuddigans." Mahoney's round face was serious, and his small eyes squinted at Jones. "They're tryin to raise apples and peaches and spuds and stuff about four miles west of town. They took that boy from the orphanage and worked him about half to death."

"Where did you hear this?"

"From Walt Hoover. He works the night shift at the mill. He seen 'em carryin' the body over to the shack, and he said the shurff told him he was sendin' for the coroner."

"They found the boy dead, is that it? And they think he was beaten to death?"

"That's the rights of it."

Marybelle Dubois came in, unpinning a heavy wool shawl and pulling it from her shoulders. "Oh no," she exclaimed when Mahoney told her what he'd heard. "That poor boy. I saw him in school a few times. They wouldn't let him go to school regularly. I heard he was from the orphanage. Oh, that's just so . . ."

Her brown eyes settled on Jones. "Did they really beat him to death?"

"I don't know," Jones confessed. "I just heard about it from Jake here."

"They're mean folks," Mahoney said. "I wonder if old Hoover got the rights of it."

Jones sat staring at the floor between his shoes, trying to let it soak in. This was the kind of rumor often heard in his hometown. The story was often changed from one storyteller to the next. The girl

65

spoke, her voice earnest:

"We have to find out, don't we, Mr. Jones? For our next issue?"

"Huh?" He looked up at her. "Oh yeah. Yes. Yes indeed. That we do. We're a newspaper and we present the news. I'll, uh, I'll go right over to the sheriff's office."

The sheriff wasn't in, but a deputy with a walrus moustache and droopy eyes told Jones the boy's body was taken to a shed near the courthouse where it was "layed out nice and purty in some hay." The sheriff was sending a message by horseback to Leadville to get the coroner to come to Maxwell and make it official, though everybody knew what happened.

"It's for shore," the deputy said with a drawl. "Old Cuddigan even admitted it when Omar pointed out the cut lip and the whip marks on the boy's back. He said the boy died after he fell out of a apple tree, but he admitted he whipped 'im."

"There are marks on the body that indicate a beating?"

"It's for shore. Old lady Cuddigan tole us all about it. The old man got mad at the kid for somethin' and hit 'im with his fists and took a buggy whip to 'im."

Jones shook his head sadly, then asked, "Where is Mr. Cuddigan now?"

"Around the corner there, locked up."

"Has he been formally charged?"

"Formally charged? Wal, I dunno. If he ain't he will be."

"How about Mrs. Cuddigan? Is she under arrest?"

"Naw. She didn't do it. It was her that came to Omar's house last night and tole 'im about it. Him and me, we went out to the farm and found where old man Cuddigan had berried the body. Old lady Cuddigan held a lantern whilst we dug 'im up."

"Good God. The man's a brute."

"For shore he is, and a lot of other things. Folks are gittin' mighty unhappy about this."

"He ought to be hung."

"He will be. We don't take kindly to killin' little kids."

"How soon can he be brought to trial? The sooner the better."

"Wal now, that I don't know. We ain't never had a trial here an' I don't know."

Sheriff Omar Schmitt came in then, heavy boots thumping on the concrete floor of the courthouse basement. He carried a Colt revolver in a leather holster on his right hip. "Mornin', Mr. Editor," he said pleasantly. "Got somethin' to put in your newspaper, ain't you."

"Yes, it seems I do, indeed." Jones got the sheriff to confirm everything the deputy had said.

"Come on back here and take a look at him," Schmitt invited.

"Well, no, I don't need to do that."

"He won't bite. They used to bust out of the old jail, but they can't get out of this one."

"How old was the boy, sheriff?"

"Mrs. Cuddigan said he was thirteen. They got him from the orphanage at Leadville, took him out to that farm and made him do a man's work."

"Where is Mrs. Cuddigan?"

"Out at the farm. Somebody has to stay there and feed the chickens and hogs and milk the cows."

"I take it she's not going to be charged, then?"

"Charged? Oh. Naw, I don't think she done any wrong, except maybe letting old Cuddigan beat the boy all the time without sayin' anything. But I think she was scared of him, too."

Jones apologized for asking so many questions, but the sheriff answered them pleasantly. "The mayor said to cooperate with you, so fire away."

When he left, Jones wondered whether he had asked all the pertinent questions or whether he would leave holes in the story he was soon to write. He wished he'd had some training in journalism.

It took him the rest of the morning to write the story of the boy found dead and buried in a shallow grave on a farm owned by Mr. and Mrs. Cuddigan, and how the sheriff arrested Mr. Cuddigan. He wrote, rewrote, edited, and rewrote again, trying to get the story just right.

It occurred to him that in a small town like Maxwell, the news would be old by the time *The Maxwell Times* went to press, but there was nothing he could do about that. In the afternoon, he picked up two more filings for mining claims. That had to go in the paper.

His next job, which he started working on early the next morning, was writing his first editorial. It had to be a good one, one that would be read by every literate person in Maxwell County.

Pencil in hand, he wrote: "With this issue begins the new *Maxwell Times*, with a new editor and publisher at the helm. *The Maxwell Times* will strive to be a representative of all the citizens, from the businessman and politician to the mill worker and miner. *The Maxwell Times* is neither Democrat nor Republican. It advocates neither the gold standard nor the silver standard. While neutral in politics, the publisher and editor believes sincerely in giving equal print to each side, and we will endeavor to expose graft or corruption in all quarters. We will dedicate ourselves to pointing out the wrongs that exist in our society, and our goal is to be an exponent of what is best for our community and to be a mirror of life."

On he wrote, stopping now and then to flex the fingers of his right hand and to sharpen his pencils. His employees had come in, said "Good morning," and gone right to work setting type.

"The publisher has an abiding faith in this region and its citizenry, and believes the Almighty God has smiled kindly upon us, creating the beautiful scenery and the precious minerals that have made Maxwell and its surroundings prosper. Though we are told that the winters are long and harsh, we are convinced that man's ingenuity will overcome all obstacles, and the threat of hardships will only bring us closer together."

At noon he went to the Iveywood, was pleasantly surprised to find ham on the menu, and had two sandwiches. The reserved table was not occupied, and he sat at the counter.

It was late afternoon when he finished the first editorial of his life, and he finished it with a plea for the citizenry to patronize the merchants of Maxwell. "It is because of their enterprising spirit and their willingness to gamble their resources in business that we do not have to travel all the way to Leadville to purchase the necessities of life."

Three days later, on Sunday morning, the new

Maxwell Times hit the streets, and it was that night that Mr. Cuddigan was taken by a group of masked men from his cell in the Maxwell County jail and hung.

Chapter Seven

Will Jones was outraged when he heard about it. It was his employee Jacob Mahoney who broke it to him. "I heard it at breakfast, boss."

"Why, this is, this is terrible. It's uncivilized. Why didn't the sheriff stop them? Why didn't they wait for the trial? That man would surely have been convicted. Why, this is, this is not the way civilized human beings behave." He looked at his two employees for agreement. Their faces showed nothing.

"Why did they have to take the law into their own hands? With all the evidence, that poor wretch would have been convicted and executed legally or sent to prison for the rest of his life."

"We ain't never had a trial here," Mahoney said.

"Mr. Jones." The girl was looking at him with those wide brown eyes. "We're not too far removed from the days of total lawlessness here, the days when the only time justice was done was when the citizens did it themselves. You see, we're not so accustomed to turning everything over to the authorities."

Again he was amazed at her eloquence.

"Um." He shoved his hands into his pockets. "But we have an elected sheriff, and we have a new courthouse. We must let the authorities take care of these things. It's the only civilized way." He didn't mean to, but he found himself close to pleading with her to agree.

"You're right, of course, Mr. Jones. But you can't reform people overnight. Perhaps when a trial is finally conducted here and the people see how the legal system works, perhaps then there will be no more vigilantism."

He pondered her words, then smiled. "Are these your thoughts, Miss Dubois, or are these the thoughts of the schoolteacher, Benjamin Tucker?"

"Excuse me," she said, turning away. "I have work to do."

For a long moment he stood there, watching her work. He had spoken with sarcasm, and he shouldn't have. She was a good and loyal employee.

He would have to make it up to her.

Sheriff Omar Schmitt wasn't too upset over the hanging. "It happens," he said. "The wheels of justice move too damn slow for some people, and sometimes the wheels don't move at all."

"Couldn't you stop them?"

"Stop them? Hell, I don't sit up here all night guardin' this jail."

"Was there no one in authority here?"

"Shore there was. But I got only one deputy, and he

has to sleep sometimes, too. That's why we got that cot in the storeroom, so one of us can get a little shut-eye when we ain't got time to go home and sleep."

"I see. They caught him asleep?"

"Shore they did. Hell, if they'd come to your house in the middle of the night they'd a caught you asleep, too. Listen, Mr. Editor, I try to keep somebody here most of the time, but sometimes we put in long days—and nights too—and it ain't no disgrace to try to rest our bones on that cot in there when we get a chance."

"Um. I see. Did your deputy get a look at them? Would he recognize them if he saw them again?"

"He looked right at 'em and right at that double-barreled scattergun one of 'em had, but their heads was covered with flour sacks, and no, he prob'ly wouldn't recognize 'em."

"It had to have been local men."

"Do you know how many men that is? Hell, I think somebody told you once there are half a dozen minin' camps in Maxwell County, and a lot of men come and go."

"Has anyone told the widow?"

"No. I'm fixin' to do that now." The sheriff hitched up his gun belt and pulled his broad-brimmed hat down tighter. "Unless you want to do it."

"Uh, no."

Will Jones wrote the story, beginning with: "Vigilante justice prevailed in Maxwell Sunday night with the death by hanging of Mr. Jerome Cuddigan, who was taken from his cell at the Maxwell County jail by ten to twelve masked men.

"Mr. Cuddigan's body was cut down from a tall spruce tree in front of the courthouse by Sheriff Omar

73

Schmitt after his deputy, Sam Courtney, awakened him at three o'clock in the morning and told him of the incident.

"Deputy Courtney related he was napping on a cot in the sheriff's office when the men shook him awake, threatened him with a double-barreled shotgun and took the key to the cell from him. Deputy Courtney stated that he was powerless to stop the vigilantes and feared for his own life. He was held prisoner in the sheriff's office until after the deed was done, and then was told to wait at least one hour before leaving the office.

"Deputy Courtney stated he was terrified of the masked men and did as ordered, fearing the man with the shotgun was waiting outside the courthouse to be certain he stayed inside for an hour."

Jones wrote two full columns for the front page and wrote another column for an inside page about the crime Mr. Cuddigan was accused of. Then he set about writing another editorial.

Headlined, "Vigilante Justice Cannot Be Condoned," the editorial blistered the "cowards in masks who took an unarmed man from his jail cell and hung him from a tree in front of the courthouse.

"This was an act of cowardice, disguised as justice," he wrote. "This kind of vigilante activity must be stopped at once, and the perpetrators must themselves be identified, arrested and brought to justice. Only, let us hope that they will not be the victims of the kind of justice they meted out to Mr. Cuddigan. Let us have them formally charged with the crime, then tried in a court of law by a panel of their peers. Only through the legal system of justice can the citizens of Maxwell

County live without fear of being victims of crime, and only through the legally constituted judiciary can differences of opinion be settled without brutality. The vigilante way is the cowardly way."

He waited until Tuesday morning to make the rounds of merchants and collect the advertising sheets. He was happy to find that he had two full pages of ads again. But he noted with disappointment that the stacks of newspapers he had left with the merchants were not depleted. The stacks were shorter, but there were a lot of newspapers left unsold.

Now that he'd solved the problem of getting enough advertising to pay the bills, he had to find a way to increase readership. He mulled it over in his mind as he walked to his office, but he could think of no way to do it.

The American Press Service in Denver had sent him enough copy in the mail to fill six pages, and he had to sort through it carefully and decide which to print and which to toss in the wastebasket. Editing a newspaper wasn't an easy job.

Writing the news wasn't getting any easier either, but he was becoming more proficient at sharpening pencils with a penknife.

The next issue of *The Maxwell Times* went to press on Saturday, and on Sunday morning Will Jones and Jacob Mahoney carried armloads of newspapers to the stores and restaurants where they were left with small handwritten signs, saying, Two Cents Each.

On Sunday afternoon Jones rented a horse and buggy from the Ardmore Livery and went for a lonely drive on a mountain road. He stopped twice to admire the scenery, the steep pine-covered hills, and shimmering aspen leaves, the boulders as big as houses, the blaze of wild flowers on the meadows, the gurgling streams. Breathtaking.

On Monday he was horsewhipped.

Chapter Eight

They came in wearing flour sacks with eye and nose holes over their heads. There were four of them.

Will Jones was sitting at his desk, writing, and his two employees were in the back end of the room, setting type.

"William Jones?"

His head came up and his eyes widened as he saw them coming toward him. "Yes."

"We're some of the citizens that you called cowards." With that the leader raised a buggy whip and brought the lash down on Jones's head.

Jones jumped up and covered his head with his arms. The lash struck again, this time on the shoulders. Jones uncovered his head and tried to grab the whip. Another lash. The tall young man felt a stinging on his right cheek. It hurt and brought tears to his eyes. He tried again to grab the whip, got it and tried to wrestle it out of the masked man's hands.

Two of the others got behind him and pinned his arms to his sides. The whip was raised again.

But it didn't descend. Suddenly a wild bear was loose among them.

With a growl, Jacob Mahoney was there, grabbing, pummeling, kicking. He got the whip wielder in a bear hug from behind, lifted his feet off the floor and swung him around in a circle.

Centrifugal force brought the man's feet up horizontally, and as Mahoney swung him around, his feet hit two of the other masked men, knocking them back.

The horsewhip was dropped, and while Jones wrestled with one of the men, the girl picked up the whip.

The struggle ended a few seconds later. Mahoney threw two of the men bodily out the door, and the girl drove the other two out, lashing furiously at them.

For a time Jones couldn't believe what had happened, and he could only stand there and stare at the open door. His mouth was open, but he was saying nothing. His right cheek stung.

Then the girl let loose a low scream, and Jones saw one of the masked men reaching inside his unbuttoned shirt, drawing a pistol from under his belt. The man's hand stopped immediately when he found himself looking into the bore of the big revolver in Mahoney's hand. The hammer was back. The gun was cocked. Mahoney said one word:

"Git."

They left, walking between two buildings, heading for the alley, cursing, threatening.

The husky printer watched until they were out of sight and turned to his employer. "Hurt you, boss?"

"Huh? Uh, no, I don't, uh, think so."

"You've got a cut on your face." The girl stood in front of him, looking up at him. "It should be attended to."

"Huh?" He fingered the wound and looked at the blood on his fingers. "It's, uh, do you know who they were?"

"I know one of 'em, boss. I didn't get a look at his face, but I know his clothes—his harness boots, and that Monkey Ward shirt with flaps on the pockets. It's that deputy, Sam Courtney."

"Are you sure?"

"That's the rights of it."

"Well, I have to . . . I have to file a complaint against him right away."

"You mean tell the sheriff to arrest him?"

"Of course. I can't let him get away with this. We have laws to protect us from this sort of thing."

"I don't know as I'd do that, boss."

"Why? That's what criminal laws are for."

"Mr. Jones." It was the girl talking. Real concern showed in her brown eyes. "You see . . . it's just not the way things are done here. You'd . . . please don't misunderstand me, but you would be laughed at."

"Laughed at. Why? Because I don't want to let someone get away with assault and battery against a law-abiding citizen? Not only that, but if he's one of the vigilantes, then he had a hand in hanging Mr. Cuddigan. He wasn't forced at gunpoint to stay out of it. He was lying."

"Mr. Jones." She wore a worry frown. "Please sit down and let me attend to that wound. I have some astringent at Mr. Tucker's house, and it will take only a few minutes to run and get it."

He put his fingers to the wound again. It stung.

"Please, sir." She pushed gently at him until he was backed up against his desk chair. "You have a cut

79

that should not be ignored. Please don't do anything until I return."

He sat, a little confused, trying to decide what to do.

"I'll be back in a few minutes, Mr. Jones." She wrapped the wool shawl around her shoulders and hurried out the door.

"Why?" Jones looked at the burly printer. "Why would I be laughed at if I reported this to the sheriff, or rather to the town marshal?"

"Marybelle's got the rights of it, boss. She can explain this stuff better than I can."

"But I don't . . ." He frowned at the floor. "I don't understand."

She was back in five minutes, out of breath from running. "Here." She showed him a small bottle with a screw cap. "This will clean the wound and prevent infection. That's our main concern now. Will you put your head back, Mr. Jones?"

He did as she asked, and she bent over him. "It will sting a little, but it will make you feel better in the long run."

Feel better? Good God, he felt better already. Her long dark hair hung down and tickled his left cheek. Her brown eyes were just a few inches above his. He looked into her face as she dabbed some astringent on a piece of cotton and admired the straight nose and the firm lips and chin. He could see and even smell the woman in her, and—good God.

She murmured, "Here we go now."

He stiffened slightly and tears came back to his eyes as the astringent took hold, but he smiled.

"There." She smiled, too. Her teeth were white

against the dark skin, and her face was only inches from his.

Good God.

Straightening, she screwed the cap back on the bottle and placed the bottle on his desk. "It's stopped bleeding. I think it will scab over soon, and it will be fine." The frown returned. "I hope it won't leave a scar."

"Thank you, Miss Dubois." The words came out weakly. He cleared his throat and tried to put some strength into his voice. "I appreciate this." Looking around at Mahoney, who was already back at work, he said, "I'm indebted to both of you. You saved me from a severe beating. I couldn't have handled them alone."

"You're welcome, Mr. Jones." She turned and went to the back of the room, back to the type cases.

At lunch he again met the lawyer, Justus DeWolfe. They sat together at a small table in a corner of the Iveywood Restaurant, and Jones told him all about it. "Maybe I could sue," Jones suggested. "If I can't get him arrested for a crime, maybe I can sue for personal injury."

"Well," the young lawyer said, chewing rapidly on a tough piece of beef, "I'll be happy to take the case if you're prepared to pay a retainer, but not on a contingency basis."

"Why not?"

Justus DeWolfe swallowed and hesitated before taking another bite. "Two things. First, I doubt your employee can positively identify this Sam Courtney.

Oh, he is probably convinced in his own mind, but making a jury believe it is something else. Boots and a shirt are not very good evidence. Second, even if we did convince a jury that Sam Courtney was one of the attackers, they wouldn't find him guilty of any wrongdoing."

"Do you mean a jury would allow someone to get away with this kind of behavior?"

The lawyer mulled it over in his mind, then answered carefully. "Considering that the attackers were driven off . . . In this place and in this time, yes. In Denver, maybe no. In the East, maybe no. But here . . ." He lifted another forkful of mashed potatoes and gravy to his mouth.

"My employees tell me I would be laughed at if I went to court."

Chewing fast and swallowing, DeWolfe said, "They're right. That's why I have to leave here and go back to Denver. I had hoped that, what with the way Maxwell is—was—growing, there would be plenty of business for an attorney here, but I was mistaken."

"You're leaving?"

"I'll have to if I want a career in law." He put his fork down and took a sip of coffee. "Mr. Jones, this is still the raw frontier. Oh, sure, we have a new courthouse and a courtroom, but no trial has ever been conducted, and people here don't think in terms of litigation. What happens is, when two or more men have a difference of opinion, they duke it out or shoot it out. Nobody hires an attorney and goes to court."

"That's terrible."

DeWolfe smiled a grim smile. "That it is. Especially for an attorney."

Jones cut off a piece of the beef, forked it into his mouth and chewed. And chewed. Finally, after he managed to swallow it, he said, "It'll change. It has to. I hate to see you leave."

"Oh, I'll stay around for a little while. My folks in Denver aren't letting me starve. My dad owns a machine shop and can afford to keep me in groceries a little longer, but unless things change soon I'll be forced to leave."

"We just have to change people's attitude."

"Right. The way things are, they think it's sissy to hire a lawyer to settle differences."

"But fighting it out or shooting it out means that whoever is the most skillful with his fists or a gun always gets his way. We have to put a stop to that."

"Well," DeWolfe said, gulping down a piece of beef, "you're a newspaper editor. You do that."

"I certainly intend to try."

"Do you want to retain me?"

"Uh, no, not this time. I guess I'll just let it pass."

The lawyer wiped his chin with a linen napkin, drained his coffee cup and stood, ready to go. He looked down at Jones. "Let me leave you with one thought. I shouldn't say this, but I know it's true. Duking it out and shooting it out more often than not results in a miscarriage of justice. But keep in mind that the good guys don't always win in court, either."

Chapter Nine

Will Jones had his second meeting with the town fathers that night. They sat at their reserved table and shook their heads sadly when he told them how he got the wound on his cheek.

"That's exactly the sort of thing we have to stop," Mayor Wilbur Osgood commented. "Your editorial was exactly right. Keep up the good work."

Jones looked at the sheriff to see whether he agreed. Omar Schmitt was nodding affirmatively. He wondered whether to tell the sheriff that his deputy was one of the vigilantes. He decided not to, not at the moment anyway.

"It was the last paragraph of your first editorial that I liked," said Oliver Scarbro. "I had customers I never saw before."

"Did our advertising prove profitable?" Jones asked.

"It did bring in a couple of people from over at Gopher Gulch," said Thom Douglas, owner of the harness and leather shop. "But only a couple."

"I don't think very many people in the mining camps read your newspaper," commented Cyrus

Dochstader, the banker.

"I'll find a way to deliver papers there," Jones promised. "I'll have to hire some people to do that." Silently, he wondered if he could afford to hire more people.

"That'd help," Scarbro said.

"Yes," the mayor put in, "we've got to find a way to bring those folks to Maxwell."

The beef served by Restaurateur Josef Grunenwald was a better quality than he served at lunch, and the canned green beans had some kind of spice added that made them a little more palatable.

Dinner over, the group adjourned to the Totten House of Spirits where Jones was persuaded to down three drinks of whiskey. It burned his throat and stomach, but he managed to keep his face straight. He thought it necessary to be one of them, to be their friend. Without their advertising the newspaper would have to close.

On his way home—back to his late uncle's house— he passed *The Times* building, saw the lamps lighted and saw through the window that his employees were working. He had an urge to open the door and shout, "Go Home," but he realized he had drunk too much and his voice was slurry, and he would probably say the wrong thing.

On Sunday, Will Jones rented a horse and buggy again, took two bundles of newspapers with him, asked directions, and drove to two of the small mining camps on the creeks that poured off the Continental Divide to the west.

The roads were barely passable, and at times he feared the buggy wheels would break or come off, or the horse wouldn't be able to pull the buggy out of the ruts and holes.

The first camp had a sign with the word Bluebird scrawled in big, uneven letters and nailed to a tree. Beyond was a collection of shacks made of logs, tarpaper, canvas, rocks, and even cardboard. The one street was pitted and rutted so badly that Jones thought it would be difficult to even walk on it.

Most of the residents were men, but there were a few women in long dresses watching him as he clucked to the horse to keep it going on the terrible road. The men were bearded with faded eyes, most wearing baggy wool pants held up by suspenders. The women had hard faces, lined, wrinkled. Their hair was pulled back and tied behind their heads. One wore a sunbonnet.

Jones said, "Whoa" to the horse, then, "hello," trying to be cheerful.

They just looked at him.

"I'm Will Jones, editor and publisher of *The Maxwell Times*. With your permission, I'd like to leave a few newspapers here for your perusal." He got down from the buggy seat and placed a tied bundle of newspapers on the ground.

A prospector with a wild beard came over and broke the heavy twine with his bare hands—which amazed Jones—took a paper off the pile and held it up in front of his eyes.

"What does it say?" The woman in a sunbonnet looked over the man's shoulder. Two more men came over and looked at the newspaper in the man's hands.

86

"Says somethin' about a hangin' over to Maxwell and the newspaper editor gettin' whupped."

"Yeah, I heered about that. They hung that kid killer."

"He won't kill no more orphans," the woman said.

Jones watched them and listened to them. He said, "All the details are there, and there is other news, too. There are some advertisements from the stores in Maxwell, and there's news about the latest mineral discoveries."

They ignored him and studied the newspaper. Another man took another paper and squinted at it. "My eyes ain't too good," he said, sadly.

"Eyes," another bearded gent chided. "You c'n spot a hint of color a mile away. You cain't read."

Another newspaper was taken from the pile, then another. "Look at this," a woman said. "They's sellin sewin' machines at the store in Maxwell. Like to get me one."

Jones watched them, smiling. "They're free for now. Complimentary. In the future we'll bring over a bundle of newspapers every Sunday which you can buy for two cents apiece."

"You're the editor?"

"Yes, I am."

"You're the one that got whupped by some a them vigilantes."

His smile slipped, but he forced it back. "I'll tell you this. They received more than they handed out."

A man laughed. "Way I heered it, old Mahoney kicked the hound dog out of 'em, and that breed gal, the purty one, took their own whip and lit into 'em till they cried for their mammies."

Laughter.

Jones laughed with them. "They got more than they bargained for."

"Surely left their tracks on your face, howsomever." A woman with a lipless mouth squinted at him.

Jones fingered the scar on his right cheek, but continued smiling. "Now I know how a horse feels."

More laughter.

"Care for a cup of java, mister?"

Jones went into a one-room tarpaper shack and sat in a chair made of one-inch boards with sections of small tree trunks for legs. A woman with straggly hair poured a cup of coffee from a large black coffeepot and set it on a table made from the same materials as the chair.

He sipped the coffee. It was strong.

"Ain't got no milk," the woman said. "I surely do miss the fresh milk and eggs we had back in Arkansas."

"You folks are from Arkansas?"

"Yeah," the man said. "We heard about folks gittin' rich out here, and we sold what little we had and loaded up a wagon and come out here. So far I've been able to pan enough gold and silver out'n Bluebird Creek to buy our vittles and that's about all."

Jones looked around the room. The bed and kitchen cupboards were made of the same materials. The floor was dirt.

"Well, I wish you luck," he said. "I've heard that some people are finding precious metals around here, but I know a lot of others are finding nothing worthwhile."

"We'll find 'er," the man said.

Draining his cup, Jones stood. "Well, I have to go. I must take some papers to another camp, one called Silverton. I'm told that if I go back down the road about a mile and take the left fork in the road I'll come to it."

"Yep."

After wishing them good luck again, Jones went looking for his horse and buggy and found that the horse had wandered down the road a short distance and was being held there by a boy in a homemade muslin shirt. "Thanks." He handed the boy two copper pennies and added another when he saw the wide smile.

It was late afternoon when he started back to Maxwell, but he was pleased with himself. It was with some trepidation that he had started his trip that day. He had often heard stories as a boy about the way some of the hill people of Missouri were hostile to strangers, and he was pleasantly surprised to find the hill people of Colorado sociable. Once they discovered he was friendly, they went out of their way to be friendly themselves.

A few miles from town he spotted a figure on horseback ahead of him and supposed it was one of the townspeople. His horse, realizing it was going back to the barn where it would be fed and get the harness off, was trotting right along. The buggy pulled closer to the figure on horseback.

It was a strange figure at first, but as Jones pulled closer he realized it was a woman. Her horse, a long-legged bay, was traveling in a slow trot, and the woman seemed perfectly comfortable on its back. When Jones got closer, she looked over her shoulder at him.

It was Marybelle Dubois.

Now that he thought about it, Jones remembered being told that the half-breed Indian girl often disappeared for a day or so on weekends. She always disappeared at night, and no one knew where she went. When anyone asked her, all they got was a smile.

She must just now be coming back from wherever she went, Jones guessed. It will be dark soon, and she must be planning to ride into town after dark.

The girl apparently didn't recognize him, and she reined her horse off the road, back among the lodgepole pines, and waited for him to pass. He brought his horse to a halt.

"Miss Dubois?"

She recognized him then and rode forward. "Evening, Mr. Jones."

"Good evening. Out riding for pleasure?"

"Yes sir. This is Mr. Tucker's horse." She wore a long, billowy dress that covered the saddle and covered her from the shoulders down, leaving only her feet in the iron stirrups exposed. She reached down and scratched the animal's neck. "He's a good horse. He'll carry anyone, or he'll pull a buggy or do whatever anyone tells him to do."

He noticed the empty burlap bags hanging down both sides of the saddle.

"Can you tie him to the back of this vehicle and

ride up here with me? It's more comfortable."

"Oh, this is fine. I don't mind at all. Do you ride, Mr. Jones?"

"Sure. A little. I used to like to ride horseback as a boy."

"It's something I enjoy. Especially on a beautiful day like today. I never get tired of being in the mountains."

He guessed it was the Indian blood in her. "It's beautiful, all right. Do you ever get lost?"

"Lost? No, there's no danger of that. I'm half Indian, you know. I was raised among Indians, and I learned to read the ground the way some kids learn to read a book. I can always follow my own tracks back if necessary."

"I envy you, Miss Dubois. I wish I could do that. I've always admired the old frontier trappers and settlers and . . ." He realized that he was about to mention Indian fighters, and he shut his mouth so fast he almost choked.

She chuckled at his embarrassment. "You know nothing about Indians, do you, Mr. Jones."

"I, uh, I'm afraid I do not. Only what I've read in the magazines."

Another chuckle. "I've seen some of those pulp magazines. You can't believe everything you read."

He had to chuckle with her. "As an editor of a newspaper I can hardly agree with that."

They were silent a moment, then she turned her horse toward Maxwell. "We're only a mile from town, and when we get there we'll have to go separate ways." She urged her mount forward. "Have a good evening, Mr. Jones."

91

He watched her go. She sat the horse well, straight up, riding comfortably as the animal shifted into a long-legged trot.

It was the next day that Will Jones uncovered his first newspaper exposé.

Chapter Ten

For the third time it was one of his employees who told him what had happened. "Bad news, boss," Mahoney said, straightening the paper cap on his head. "Two men killed at the Bijou Mine. Hoist broke or somethin'."

"What? Two men killed? When?"

"A couple hours ago. Night shift was comin' up top when she broke. Two men in the skip. Both of 'em dead."

"Oh my," the girl exclaimed. "I saw people talking excitedly when I walked over here."

"I must . . . I must find out what happened." Jones slapped his fedora hat on his head and started out the door. He spun around, came back to his desk, grabbed a sheaf of copy paper from his desk and started out the door again. He stopped, came back and grabbed a pencil from his desk.

Sheriff Omar Schmitt wasn't in his office and neither was his deputy. Jones left the courthouse and headed for the livery, planning to rent a horse and buggy and go out to the mine. It occurred to him that boarders at the Hansen House knew the news before he did, and probably heard more than he did. He would have to find some piece of information, something interesting, that they wouldn't hear around the dining room table.

"Hey, mister."

Jones stopped and looked back. A bearded man wearing suspender overalls was approaching.

"Mister, are you the editor of *The Times*?"

"Yes sir, I am."

"Let me tell you somethin'. I don't want my name in the paper or nothin', but I can tell you more about that wreck at the Bijou than you'll get from the law."

"Oh really?" Jones stood still, waiting for the miner to continue.

"You won't put my name in the paper, will you?"

"Not if you don't want it there."

"All right, here's the real skinny. That hoist cable was worn plum through, and the shifters knowed it. There's men that complained to 'em, ever' one of 'em, and nothin' was done about it. That cable was worn out and when she snapped, it dropped the skip about a hunnerd feet and killed the two men in it."

"Hoist?"

"Shore. Don't you know nothin' about minin'?"

"I, uh, must confess I've never been in a mine."

"Well, they got a hoist and a steam engine that lowers men and ore buckets down in the hole. The hoist man knowed about that cable, too, and he complained to the shifters, too, but nobody done nothin' about it."

"Shifters?"

"Shift bosses."

"Um. I see. Then the two men who were killed were being lowered into the mine when the cable broke and dropped them about a hundred feet."

"Keereck. Only they was comin' up top. They was muckin' a drift at the bottom and was comin' up at the end of their shift."

"Did you tell the sheriff about this?"

"Shore. A bunch of us did. But he won't do nothin'."

"How do you know he won't?"

"He's a company man. He'll do what they tell 'im to do."

"Really?"

"You'll find out." The miner squinted at him with faded eyes. "Unless you're a company man, too."

"Oh no. I know nothing about the company. It's called Bijou Mining and Smelter Inc., isn't it?"

"I don't know about that ink business, but that's what it's called."

"I have learned that one company owns the mine and smelter, and the Bijou is the biggest mine around here."

"Keereck. Are you gonna put this in your newspaper?"

"Well, I don't know. If I can confirm it, yes. You bet."

"Ask anybody that works in the Bijou. We knew somebody was gonna get killed."

"I will. I certainly will."

At the livery barn, Jones was told that no horse was available that morning. The mine was only two miles away, he was told. He set out walking with a sheaf of copy paper in his hip pocket and a lead pencil in his shirt pocket.

On the way he passed two horse-drawn buggies and two men walking. Everyone said, "Howdy," or Good

95

mornin'," but that was all. After he had walked about a mile and a half on a narrow, rocky road in dense woods, he saw two more men approaching on foot from the opposite direction, and they appeared, from their dirty faces and clothes, to be mine employees.

"Pardon me, gentlemen," he said when they were close enough.

They stopped and stared at him.

"Allow me to introduce myself. I'm William Jones, editor and publisher of *The Maxwell Times*. Are you by any chance employed at the Bijou Mine?"

"Yeah."

"I wonder if I might ask you a few questions about the, uh, fatal accident."

"What questions?"

"I'm told that the accident was caused by a worn cable. Is that right?"

"That's right, mister."

"Are you sure?"

"No doubt. You can see for yourself. Anybody can see."

"Did anyone mention the worn cable to the, uh, management? I mean before the accident?"

"Yeah. They knew about it."

"Thank you very much. Good day."

The Bijou Mine consisted of two wooden buildings and a steam engine. A tall head frame with a huge pulley at the top came out of the smaller building, which was open on one side, and iron rails ran from there to the smelter about two hundred yards east.

The only person Jones recognized was Sheriff Schmitt. The sheriff met him as he approached. "Mornin', Mr. Editor. You walkin'?"

"Yes. I had no alternative. Tell me, Mr. Schmitt, what caused the accident?"

"It was a cable clamp. A double clamp. It has teeth and a couple of U bolts. The nuts came loose on the U bolts."

"Cable clamp?"

"Yeah. That's what holds the end of the cable to the hook. It's the miners' job to see that the threaded nuts are tight. When the threads don't hold, the clamp don't hold."

"I see." He wondered whether he should mention a worn cable. He decided to keep it to himself for the time being. Was the sheriff really a company man? "Can I have a look?"

"I reckon. Nothin' to see. We took the bodies out."

"What's going on in there?" Jones pointed to the larger building where one man had just left and another had just entered.

"That's the hoist house."

"I see. That's where the hoist operator works, isn't it?"

"That's right."

"Thank you, Mr. Schmitt." Jones went over to the building, opened the door and peered inside. He saw two men, one in miner's overalls and a greasy cap on his head and the other in high lace-up boots, green corduroy breeches, and a campaign hat. The workman sat in a wooden chair mounted on a platform behind a machine with two six-feet-high cog wheels and a large spool of cable between them. Two long levers came out of the bottom of the machine within easy reach of the operator, and a steam pipe ran from the machine along the wooden floor and through the

97

wall to the steam boiler out back. The workman had his hands on the levers and was looking through a large open window into the open side of the headframe building.

"Pardon me, are you employees of the mine?"

"What do you want, mister?" asked the man in the campaign hat.

Jones stepped inside. "I'm William Jones, editor and publisher of *The Maxwell Times*. I'm trying to find out what happened."

"Oh. A reporter. Well, the sheriff can tell you."

"I was wondering if you had received any complaints of a worn cable?"

"A what? Hell no. Ask the sheriff. He'll tell you it was the clamp that came loose and dropped the skip. It's the men's responsibility to check the equipment." He spoke with authority, and Jones guessed he was part of management. An engineer, perhaps.

"I see. Well, I apologize for asking this, but may I see the cable?"

"Look, mister, the cable is wound up on this spool, and we can't unwind it just so you can look at it."

"I don't mean to be presumptuous, but may I see the broken clamp?"

"It isn't broken. We put her together again with lock washers, and she's down in the shaft. She won't come loose again. Every man who gets in the skip will cast an eye on that clamp from now on."

Jones turned his attention to the man in miner's clothes. "Are you by any chance the hoist operator?" The man, with a pockmarked face, obviously the victim of chicken pox as a child, cast nervous glances at the other men and at Jones.

"Yeah."

"May I ask, have you heard any complaints of a worn cable?"

"Uh, no." Without conviction. Then louder. "No sir."

"I see. Um." He didn't want to be obvious about it, but he let his gaze stay on the spool of cable for several moments. There were a few broken strands of steel wire on the cable. The broken ends were bent back.

"That doesn't mean a thing," said the man in corduroy.

"There are always a few broken strands in any cable, but there are a million strands there. A few more or less doesn't make any difference."

"I see. Tell me, is the mine operating today?"

"Sure. We pulled the cable out and locked on another skip. "That's how we got the bodies out."

A small bell hanging over the hoist operator's head rang once, and the operator pulled a lever and started the spool of cable unwinding. Another ring, and he pulled the other lever and stopped the spool.

Jones guessed that the bell was rigged so men in the mine could signal the operator with it. But he didn't have to guess at whether the cable was worn. The section that was unwound had more broken strands.

"Well," he said, "thank you very much, gentlemen." He started to leave, then turned back. "Can you tell me whether the two victims have families?"

"They both have—had," said the man in breeches and campaign hat. "I don't know much about them, however."

Again Jones turned to the hoist operator, believing that he would know more about his fellow employees.

99

"Do you happen to know, sir?"

"Yeah, Meecham had a wife and two kids, and I think Smitty was just married last winter."

"Are they living in Maxwell?"

"Yes sir, they are."

He turned to the other man. "Can you tell me, does the company have any insurance on the employees?"

"Insurance? That's their responsibility. We pay them two-twenty a shift, and they can buy their own insurance."

"I see. Thank you very much."

Outside, Jones looked around and didn't see the sheriff. He had hoped he might bum a ride back to town in the sheriff's buggy. Well, he would have to walk. He wished he had some hiking boots or shoes with thick soles to protect his feet from the rocks.

He no more than got into the pine and spruce, out of sight of the mine buildings, when he heard some-one call in a loud whisper.

"Oh, mister."

Looking around, Jones saw the man standing in the woods near the road. He appeared to be ready to duck behind a large spruce.

"Yes?"

"You're that editor feller, ain't you?" The man continued whispering. He, too, wore miner's clothes.

"I am."

"C'mere a minute. I got somethin' to tell you."

Jones stepped over close to the man. The man's eyes were glancing around fearfully.

"I don't know what they told you, but you can't believe 'em. That clamp was all right. It was easy for 'em to loosen the nuts and tell ever'body they came

100

loose by theirselves."

"Was the cable broken?"

"You betcha ass it was. I seen it. About twenty feet from the end."

"Where is it?"

"I dunno. They took a hacksaw and cut off the busted end and hid it somewhere, but I saw it."

"Why didn't the hoist man tell me that?"

"Old Hershey? He's scared of losin' his job."

"I see. Tell me something. If I print in the newspaper that two deaths occurred because of a broken cable—because of negligence on the part of the company management—would the employees back me up? I mean, if it came to a court battle, would you testify to what you just told me?"

The man's eyes were still furtive. "I can't promise you that, mister. We all need our jobs. I got to git back."

"Then if I print what you've told me, you won't back me up."

"Sorry, mister. I should of kept my trap shut. I got to get back. I waited for you here 'cuz I thought you'd want to know the facts, but I got to git back now." He turned to go, then stopped. "I oughta warn you. If you make the company mad, they'll git you."

"Get me?"

"Yeah. Old John Pope don't say much, but he's a mean sonofabitch."

Chapter Eleven

Jones watched the man leave, walking through the trees, staying off the road, looking around furtively. He disappeared inside the head-frame building. With sudden resolve, the tall young man turned and walked back up the road to the mine.

Workmen came and went, and they squinted at him, but no one challenged his right to be there. He heard the hoist squeak on the tall head frame and saw the pulley turning. He stepped inside the head-frame building and watched in fascination as a deep iron bucket appeared out of a large hole in the ground. The hole was surrounded by a wooden platform. Two men pushed and pulled the bucket away from the shaft and dumped its contents of broken rock into a heave ore cart on flanged wheels. The wheels were sitting on rails.

Without thinking about what he was doing, Jones hurried to the ore bucket before it was lowered into the shaft again and took a close look at the end of the cable hooked over the bucket bail.

The cable was old, no doubt about that, with broken strands of steel all along. And, Jones discovered when he got close, the end had been freshly cut. The end was shiny while the rest of the cable was black from use. The clamp which held the cable doubled back, forming a loop around a large steel hook on the heavy iron bail, was rusty, but he could see where it had been recently oiled.

"Hey." It was the man in lace-up boots and corduroys coming through the open side of the building. "Get away from there. What the hell are you doing here anyway?"

"I'm, uh, just satisfying my curiosity," Jones replied, straightening up to his full height and looking down at the man.

When the man discovered he had to look up at Jones, his attitude changed immediately. "Well, you can get hurt standing there, and we don't any more people hurt. You'll have to leave. Company rules."

"Yeah," Jones said. "Sure." He left, walking briskly toward the road.

It was decision time. Will Jones worried about it all the way back to town. At noon, he went to the Iveywood, hoping to find the young lawyer, Justus DeWolfe, there, but had to eat lunch alone. The reserved table was unoccupied.

After lunch he went back to his desk, sat and drummed the desktop with his fingers, listened to Jacob Mahoney's tuneless whistling, and then went to the lawyer's office. He found the young man sitting tilted back in his chair with his feet on his desk. The feet came down when Jones entered, but went back up when Justus DeWolfe recognized him.

"Still no work, Mr. DeWolfe?"

"Naw."

"Hear about the accident at the Bijou Mine?"

"Yeah."

"I'm no lawyer, but it seems to me there might be some business there."

"How?"

"I've been told by two—no three—different employees of the mine that the deaths were caused by negligence on the part of management."

The feet came down again, and the lawyer put his elbows on the desk and looked intently at Jones. "Really? Tell me about it."

Jones sat and told him.

"You say the cable broke near the end and they cut off the broken end?"

"It looked that way to me."

DeWolfe started shaking his head. "Won't work."

"Why?"

"How could I prove it?"

"Get them on the witness stand, under oath. The employees will testify, too. You can make them testify. I'm no lawyer, but I know that much. And I can tell about what I saw."

"Won't work. First, it would be the miners' word against the testimony of professional men, and what you saw doesn't mean anything. Second, who would pay me? I can't work for nothing, and believe me, it would take a lot of work."

"The miners have a good case. If you win, you'll win a lot of money."

DeWolfe shook his head again. "If I'm engaged to handle litigation over this, I'll have to work for the mine owners. They could come in here and lay some money on this desk. If I represented the employees without a retainer, which I doubt they can pay, I wouldn't get a cent until the whole thing was over and the judgement paid. That is, if I won. Management can hire a lawyer, pay him well, and that lawyer can file motion after motion and keep the case out of the courts for a year at least, and by that time the employees would have been fired or persuaded to quit and move on, or their memories would have dimmed or . . ." The lawyer shrugged. "Not only that, the company's lawyer would move for a change of venue and get it. It would be extremely difficult to find a dozen impartial jurors in Maxwell County."

"In other words the trial, if there were one, would be conducted elsewhere."

"No doubt about it. And somewhere far away. It would be damned expensive."

"I see." Jones looked down at his shoes. They were scuffed and dirty. "I know now what you meant the other day."

"What? When?"

"At lunch. You said the good guys don't always win in court."

"It's sad but true. I might be the only lawyer in the country who'll admit it."

"Well, thanks for your time." Jones stood and put on his hat.

"Are you going to print what the employees told you?"

"I'm considering it."

"You could be sued. John Pope, owner of the Bijou, is a man who . . . I've got a hunch, just a hunch, that he's vindictive as hell."

"But dammit." Jones sat down again. "A newspaper's duty is to print the truth. Are we, the editors and reporters, going to let the fear of litigation deter us from our duty?"

"Let me give you some free advice. The law isn't all bad. The lawmakers have a duty, too, and that is to protect the innocent from blatant, careless, irresponsible journalism. And I'll tell you something else. Even if you can prove that every word you print is the truth and you printed it without malice, it will still cost you a lot of money to protect yourself from a lawsuit. Even if you win you lose."

Now that he was thinking about it, Jones knew the lawyer was right. He mulled it over in his mind and said, barely audibly, "Maybe . . . maybe it's better to just duke it out."

His feet were sore from walking on the rocky road to the mine in thin-soled shoes, and he wished, as he walked back to his office, that some divine wisdom would strike him from above and tell him what to do.

At the office, he found Jacob Mahoney at work, but the girl, Marybelle Dubois, was missing.

"She went to Mr. Tucker's house where she's been stayin'," Mahoney explained. "Mr. Tucker's gittin' sicker all the time. She'll be back."

"Oh. Well, I hope Mr. Tucker gets better."

"He ought to be in a hospital."

"Then why isn't he?"

"He won't go. Knows he dyin' and wants to stay here."

"Is there no doctor in Maxwell?"

"There is. Doc Manley. He's over to Mr. Tucker's house, too."

"Well, I hope he recovers." Jones went back to worrying about his own problem. He took a piece of newsprint and started writing, just as an experiment.

"Two employees of the Bijou Mine were killed Monday when a cable broke and dropped their conveyance about one hundred feet to the bottom of the mine shaft."

Could he prove the cable broke? Yes, if he could get the miners to testify. They could be subpoenaed and ordered to testify. And if he wrote what the sheriff said, about a loosened clamp being responsible for the deaths, every working man in Maxwell County would know he was just taking the easy way out and wasn't telling everything. They would have no confidence in the press, and he wouldn't blame them.

But the working men wouldn't pay for his defense if he were sued for libel.

For an hour Jones sat at his desk, worrying. He put on his hat and went out onto the plank sidewalk, worrying. He walked, sore feet and all, around the block and back to his office. Inside he picked up his pencil and wrote:

"Sheriff Omar Schmitt blamed the deaths of two employees of the Bijou Mine on a loosened cable clamp, which allowed the end of the hoist cable to slip and drop the employees' conveyance, called a skip, to the bottom of the mine shaft.

"Sheriff Schmitt said threaded nuts which hold the clamp together had worked themselves loose and thus the clamp failed to hold the doubled end of the cable

107

in place."

In the next paragraph he named the dead men and their families and realized he would have to add something about their funerals, or funeral plans.

Marybelle Dubois came in then, breathless from hurrying. "I'm sorry, Mr. Jones. I'll work later tonight to make up for it."

He looked up from his desk. "No need to, Miss Dubois. How is Mr. Tucker?"

"Bad." She shook her head sadly. "The doctor visited him and said there is nothing he can do without sending him to the hospital at Leadville."

"But he doesn't want to go?"

"No sir. He said he doesn't want to die in a hospital."

"Then there's really nothing anyone can do, is there. Tell me, I should have asked sooner, but I wonder, is his illness tuberculosis?"

"Yes sir. It's not the same kind of consumption the miners get. All anyone can do for him is try to make his last days comfortable. I'll work late to make up for taking the time."

"Miss Dubois, is there any other way we can get out the paper? I mean without your having to work late?"

"No sir."

"Yes there is, boss." Mahoney looked across the room at them. "I can work late, too. Twixt the two of us, we'll get 'er out."

"But you're already working twelve hours a day, six days a week."

"There's more hours in a day than that, boss, and there's seven days in a week."

"Why?" Jones found it hard to believe. "I'm told

108

the miners work ten-hour shifts and get two dollars and twenty cents a day. Why are you willing to work so hard for less pay?"

"We believe in this newspaper, Mr. Jones." Her brown eyes held steady. "Your uncle lectured us about the importance of journalism, and we believed him."

She wasted no time in getting back to her type cases and going to work, moving as fast as her fingers and eyes allowed.

"Well, I'll be darned," Jones muttered, turning back to the story he was writing. It was then that he reached his decision. He wrote:

"Some employees of the mine attributed the deaths to a badly worn hoist cable, which they said parted about twenty feet from where it was held together by the clamp. They stated that they had been fearful of the cable for some time and had complained to the managers of the Bijou Mine and Smelter Co. on several occasions about it. The employees wish to be anonymous, fearing for their jobs, and in this article they shall remain nameless.

"They advised this reporter that the company managers ignored their complaints until eventually the cable became so badly worn that it parted, allowing the conveyance to fall. It is feared that if the cable is not replaced, other accidents will occur and more employees will be injured or killed."

When he finished he handed the copy to Jacob Mahoney with instructions to set it in type as soon as possible, just in case he was tempted to change his mind. Mahoney read it over and whistled.

"Man oh man. This is dealin' aces right off the top, boss. Ever'body knows what's goin' on at the Bijou, but this'll be the first time anybody says it out loud."

Marybelle Dubois read over Mahoney's shoulder. "It's common knowledge that working conditions are not safe there, but this will be the first time it is said publicly."

"Man oh man," Mahoney added, "this'll set this town on its ear."

"Yeah," Jones mumbled, worrying again, "that's just what I'm afraid of."

Chapter Twelve

When the paper hit the street it caused excitement. Will Jones and Jacob Mahoney left stacks of newspapers in the restaurant, the mercantile, on the sidewalk in front of the Totten House of Spirits, and in front of the drugstore. Each stack had a rock on top to keep the papers from blowing away and a cigar box with a cardboard sign reading, Two Cents Each.

The citizens of Maxwell gathered around, dropped pennies in the cigar boxes and picked papers off the stacks. They talked animatedly with each other and shook their heads. Jones knew that what they were reading really wasn't news to them, but they were surprised to be reading it.

They looked at him curiously when he approached on the boardwalk, and stepped back to make room for him to pass. "Mornin', Mr. Editor," someone said. Others just looked at him.

At the Iveywood, he saw no one he recognized, and sat at the counter.

"We're out of eggs again," he was told. "Flapjacks and boar belly."

"That'll be fine." Anything would be better than

his own cooking, he had decided.

When he went to his office on Monday he found his two employees working and Maggie Hansen waiting for him.

"Good morning, Mrs. Hansen," he said pleasantly.

She was dressed in a white outfit with white gloves. Her brown hair was pinned high on her head, and she carried a white parasol. A handsome woman, he realized. A widow. If he were nearer her age, he might—

"Good morning, Mr. Jones. I wonder if I might talk to you. I know you're a busy man, but I'll only take a few minutes of your time."

"Certainly."

She was already seated in the barrel chair beside his desk, and he folded himself into the desk chair and faced her. "What would you like to talk about?"

"Prices, Mr. Jones."

"Prices?"

"Yes, prices. I wonder if you know how much we have to pay for groceries here in Maxwell."

"Well, no. I've been taking my meals at the Ivey-wood."

"Did, you, by any chance, on your journey to Maxwell, stop in Leadville? Or Denver?"

"Why yes, of course. I had to change trains in Denver and take a stage from Leadville. I had to wait in both cities."

"Did you happen to buy anything there?"

"Only a few meals. Why?"

"Did you pay as much there as you do at the Iveywood?"

"Well no. I'll admit I was surprised at the prices at

112

the Iveywood."

"It's that way everywhere, Mr. Jones. They're robbing us, and your newspaper is helping them do it."

"Well now . . ." He stroked his moustache with a thumb and forefinger and pondered what she had said. "Mrs. Hansen, would you explain that?"

"The advertisements you print. They always advertise something that looks like a fair price. So we go there and find out that that is the only item that is priced fairly. The advertising that you print is a come-on."

"Well, you have to consider the cost of doing business in Maxwell, Mrs. Hanson. In places like Leadville, supplies and merchandise are delivered by railroad. Everything that comes here has to be unloaded from the railcars, reloaded into wagons and hauled by horsepower. It costs more to do business here."

"Does it have to cost twice as much?"

"Twice as much?"

"Yes. I correspond by mail with friends in Leadville, and last spring I went by stage to Leadville to visit them. Prices of almost everything are twice as high in Maxwell as they are there."

Jones was silent, thinking about what she had said.

"Not only that, but since they started advertising again in *The Times*, prices have gone even higher. People in the placer camps have been coming here instead of Leadville because Maxwell is closer and because your newspaper advertises fair prices."

"Are you saying, Mrs. Hansen, that advertising in the newspaper pulls them into Maxwell where they are gouged, if you'll pardon the expression."

"Gouged is exactly right. I'm paying so much for groceries that I'm being forced to charge more for meals at the Hansen House. I hate to do that, but I have to."

All he could do was shake his head.

"They talk about how Maxwell is growing, but it's only the population that's growing. There hasn't been a new store or a new business in Maxwell for over a year. What we need is some competition among the merchants."

"Um. Well, it's an economic fact that when someone has a monopoly he can do things pretty much his way."

"My late husband was an educated man, too, Mr. Jones. He was a mining engineer before he discovered gold himself and opened the Maggie Mine. He always said that competition is what keeps businessmen honest."

"That's the theory, yes. Um. Another mercantile might make a difference."

She stood and smoothed down her long skirt. "Well, I won't take any more of your time. We don't, any of us, blame you. I just thought you'd like to know."

"Please, Mrs. Hansen, don't leave just yet."

She sat again.

"Let me ask you. Do you have any idea why there have been no new stores opened here recently?"

"Of course. It's like you said. It costs too much to open a business here, but it's not just the transportation, it's the price of building lots."

"Building lots?"

"You see, Mr. Jones, about five men own most of the town of Maxwell. They bought the land and had it incorporated. When people come here to work in the mines and the smelter, they have to pay high prices for a lot to build a house on or they're paying high rent. A three-room house rents for forty dollars."

"Why don't they build outside the town limits?"

"Water."

"Pardon me?"

"Like I said, my husband was an engineer, and he told me about such things. Let me try to remember how he explained it. You see, the town sits over a fault. That is an underground cave where water collects. You can drill a well anywhere over that fault and you'll hit water in a hundred feet or less. Drill anywhere outside it and all you'll find is dry granite. It took a lot of dry holes to convince people of that."

"Uh-huh," said Jones. "So the people who own the town lots control the water. Anyone who wants to build around here has to build over that fault. And that means those five people can charge any price they want for a building lot."

"And they charge too much. There's talk about diverting water from Bluebird Creek, but nobody has been willing to put up the money it would cost. If the town grows, we'll all have to pay taxes to do that."

"Uh-humm. Uh, did you say your husband died last winter?"

"Yes. It was an accident. An ore wagon turned over on him."

"Oh. I'm sorry."

"He was riding with a load of ore in a snowstorm, coming down a hill, going to the Bijou smelter. They

115

had the wheels chain-locked." When she saw the puzzled expression on his face, she explained, "It's a way of wrapping a chain around the rear wheels and tying it to the front wheels to keep them from sliding on the snow downhill."

"Oh."

"The chain broke, and the wagon slid around and turned over and dumped the ore into a gully beside the road. Poor Bertrum was dragged under the wagon. He had a terrible head wound and never regained consciousness. The driver managed to jump off the opposite side."

"I'm terribly sorry, Mrs. Hansen."

"Mr. Pope, the gentleman who owns the Bijou, had offered to buy the Maggie, and when my husband died I sold it to him. Him and Wilbur Osgood, the mayor. They might have other partners, too, but nobody knows for sure."

"But you kept your home and turned it into a boardinghouse?"

"Yes. At first I thought I'd leave, but then I saw a need for a boardinghouse where working men could live without having to pay an arm and a leg, and I have enough help that I don't have to do much of the work, and I'm not lonely this way."

She stood again, and he walked to the door with her. "I do thank you for coming in, Mrs. Hansen, and I will give some thought to what you said. I believe, and my Uncle Nathan believed, that a newspaper belongs to the people."

"You're an honest man, Mr. Jones. You've proven that. And I want to invite you again to take your meals at the Hansen House. My customers are all

116

laboring men, but they are gentlemen. There's no swearing or bad manners at the Hansen House. I won't allow it."

"Um."

"I can't take on any more roomers now, but I'll always set a place at the table for you."

"Thank you very much." He watched her walk away, back straight, head up. A lady.

At his desk he doodled on some newsprint. What Mrs. Hansen said was true. She didn't just make it up. A person expects to pay more in an isolated town like Maxwell, but twice as much? He wondered what he could do about it.

Chapter Thirteen

Faces at the reserved table in the Iveywood weren't friendly. Conversation ceased for a moment when Will Jones entered, pulled out a chair and sat. "Good evening, gentlemen," he said. A cloud of cigar smoke hung over the table.

Finally Mayor Wilbur Osgood said, "Mr. Jones, we're conducting a meeting here of the Maxwell town council."

"Oh." Jones pondered that and almost apologized. But, after thinking for a second, he said, "I, uh, believe town council meetings are public meetings, are they not?"

They all looked hard at him, and he could feel that he was definitely an unwanted intruder. He kept his seat. Sheriff Omar Schmitt scowled at him and was next to speak.

"You made me out a fool in that newspaper of yours."

"Oh no, Mr. Schmitt, I merely relayed what information I gleaned from employees at the Bijou Mine. It seems to me that their side of the story deserves to be told."

"They don't know what they're talkin' about. I saw that cable and that clamp."

"Did you by any chance see the end of the cable?"

Omar Schmitt half rose from his seat. "You're damn right I saw it, and I don't need no newspaper editor to tell me what to look at."

"If there is anything you want to say to the public, Mr. Schmitt, I'll be glad to relay it."

"What I got to say I'm sayin' to you. You better be careful what you put in that goddamned newspaper."

John Pope, owner of the Bijou, scowled at Jones but said nothing.

"Gentlemen, gentlemen." Mayor Osgood's face was red and getting redder. "Let us hold our tempers here. This is a meeting of the Maxwell town council, and we have some business to conduct." He stuck his cigar stubb in his mouth and blew two quick puffs of smoke.

The sheriff settled down in his chair, and Jones deliberately looked away from him. There were seven men at the table, including himself, and he guessed that the town council was comprised of five men— four businessmen and the mayor, who apparently was an investor.

"Now," Wilbur Osgood said, shuffling through a sheaf of papers on the table. "We have several matters to consider. First, there is a letter from a Mrs. Doolittle in Leadville who wants to open a liquor establishment on Courtney Street. Is there any discussion?"

"What do you know about her, sheriff?" The question came from the banker, Cyrus Dochstader.

"She's a whore. Ever'body in Leadville knows her.

119

She's got a whorehouse there, and now she wants to open another here. Sell her a lot and she'll bring in the whores."

"We don't want Maxwell to become that kind of town," the mayor said. "Anyone in favor of selling her a place to build?"

No one spoke.

"Anyone opposed?"

It was unanimous.

"Now then." The mayor picked up another paper. "We have here an application from a Nathaniel Martin of Denver to open a general store in Maxwell." The mayor studied the paper, turned it over and studied it further. "Doesn't say where in Maxwell. Wherever he can find a place, I reckon."

"Does he say what he wants to sell?"

"Let's see. Yes, he lists groceries, dry goods, hardware, and miscellaneous."

"He'll be competing with me for business," said Oliver Scarbro, mercantile owner. He shot a glance at Jones.

"Yes, he will indeed," the mayor said. "But gentlemen, this is a free enterprise country. Apparently he has a legitimate plan, and he's willing to pay for a building lot. We can't keep the competition away." He, too, shot a glance at Jones.

"Sooner or later, we'll have another store in Maxwell." It was the restaurateur, Josef Grunenwald, speaking. "What with the smelter expanding and the sawmill adding another blade, more timber being cut and more mines opening up, we'll have to have more stores."

"What would you say if somebody wanted to open

120

another restaurant?" asked Scarbro.

"So be it. That's what the free enterprise system is all about."

Jones was busy taking notes.

"I'm glad to see you're getting this all down, Mr. Jones," said the mayor.

"Yes," Jones said. "This is something the citizens don't hear on the streets."

"Well then, is there any further discussion? No? Any opposition? Mr. Scarbro?"

"Naw, I guess I can't honestly vote against it," said Scarbro. He stretched his neck to see what Jones was writing. "The name is S-c-a-r-b-r-o."

"Thank you."

"Now, we have to approve pay vouchers for the city employees."

"Mr. Mayor." Jones was stretching his neck, too, now, trying to read the letter from Denver. "Did this Mr. Martin list his mailing address?"

"Why?"

"I'd, uh, just like to know. It's public business, you know."

"Very well, here." The mayor handed the paper to Jones who copied the address.

There was little further discussion of town business, and dinner was served. It was fried chicken, mashed potatoes, and brown gravy.

"My compliments," quipped Cyrus Dochstader. "This is delicious. Where did you get the chicken?"

"From the widow, Cuddigan. She's got a hired man out there now, and they're raising a few crops, and they've got those Rhode Island Reds inside a big chicken wire fence where the coyotes can't get at

121

them."

"What does she feed them?"

"Oh, they raised a little Indian corn last summer. It seems to be good chicken feed. Good cow feed, too."

"Does she have eggs to sell?"

"Yeah, but that woman at the Hansen House gets most of them. She's been a customer of the Cuddigans for years."

"Uh, Mr. Jones." The owner of the harness and leather shop was looking at him. "My ads in your newspaper brought in a little more business for awhile, but I haven't seen any of the camp people for a couple of weeks now."

Mercantile owner Oliver Scarbro added, "That advertising I'm paying for isn't bringing in much business."

Jones considered suggesting that he price his goods to compete with the stores in Leadville, but he kept his thoughts to himself. "Now that another mercantile is to open soon, you'll need to advertise more than ever."

"Yeah," he answered sourly. "Competition is good for the newspaper business."

After everyone was stuffed, the meeting was adjourned. Mayor Osgood picked up the check, looked at it and signed it. "It's the least the citizens can do for us," he said. "After all, we serve for nothing."

"I'll pay for mine," Jones said, reaching for his wallet.

Jones left the meeting feeling good. Competition was coming. Prices would be forced down to a competitive level, and advertising would pick up. Once word spread that Maxwell was growing in population more and more merchants and craftsmen would move in. Just to satisfy his curiosity Jones decided to write a letter to Nathaniel Martin of Denver and try to learn more about his plan to open a new store.

The only dark spot in the evening's events was the anger the sheriff had displayed. He needed the sheriff as a source of news. But, come to think of it, the sheriff was elected, and if he planned to run for reelection he needed the support of the newspaper. They needed each other. Unless Omar Schmitt was just plain stupid he'd make an effort to get along with the editor of the only newspaper in town. Yes, things looked good.

That is, until he made his rounds next morning to pick up the advertising sheets.

"Can't do it anymore," said the owner of the harness and leather shop. "No legal notices this week," said the county clerk. "Advertising brought a few folks in from the camps," said Oliver Scarbro, "but business hasn't picked up any."

"You've got the only store in town now," Jones argued, "and you get all the business from the town people. But with competition coming, you'll need to advertise."

"Well, I'll wait till the competition gets here, and then I'll think about it."

He couldn't understand it. They all had seemed a little withdrawn for awhile last night, but not downright unfriendly. Except the sheriff. The sheriff didn't advertise. Someone did mention that the rural people weren't coming to Maxwell. Still, they shouldn't just stop advertising all at once. Taper off, maybe, but not all at the same time.

The newspaper couldn't survive without advertising. What was going on?

Chapter Fourteen

The only good news was that four hundred pounds of newsprint he had paid for had finally arrived, along with four thirty-gallon drums of ink. They had supplies. But only one printer.

Jacob Mahoney greeted him with a long face as soon as he came in the door.

"Mr. Tucker died, boss. Marybelle is all busted up about it. She's helping take care of the body, but she said she'd be here sometime this mornin'."

Jones slumped in his desk chair. "It probably doesn't matter. We may be out of business soon anyway. The merchants have withdrawn their advertising again."

"It's that article you wrote, boss. About the mine wreck. They're all in cahoots around here."

"Why do you say that?" Jones looked up at his employee.

"Ever'body knows it, but nobody knows how."

"Would you explain that?"

Mahoney sat his wide bottom in the barrel chair. "All I know is what ever'body knows. The bigshots in this town are thicker than molasses. Some folks say the Bijou company owns this town, but nobody knows for shore."

Jones leaned forward, elbows on his knees, and looked into the printer's round face. "Tell me what you do know, Jake. Tell me what you suspect."

"I don't know much, boss, except that ever'thing costs more around here, and some folks blame it on the mine company."

"Yes, I've been told about high prices. So why do people come here?"

"The company pays good wages. Folks in Leadville hear about the Bijou payin' two-twenty a shift, and they come here to get the jobs. Only once they get here, they find out they have to pay more for a house and grub and ever'thing else."

"Why am I just now hearing about this?"

"DamfIknow, boss. I reckon it's because you spend your time—your sociable time, I mean—with the town bigshots. It's the workin' men that'll tell you what's goin' on."

"Um. So if the Bijou is paying better wages than most mining companies, then why are people blaming them?"

The printer shrugged his big shoulders. "We don't know much about it. All we know is somebody's dealin' busted flushes."

"And you suspect the Bijou is responsible?"

"We ain't shore we've got the rights of it, but that's what some folks think."

Jones leaned back in the chair, looked at the ceiling and thought it over. "Well, it certainly sounds like there's some sort of price collusion going on in Maxwell."

"A which?"

"Price collusion. That's when the merchants get together and decide among themselves what prices they're going to charge. I've read in the Kansas City papers that someone in Washington wants to make that illegal."

Marybelle Dubois was wearing black when she came to work late that day, and Will Jones greeted her as soon as she stepped across the threshold.

"No need for you to work today, Miss Dubois. I'm very sorry to hear that Mr. Tucker passed away. Take the day off. Take whatever time you need to do whatever you have to do."

Her eyes were red rimmed, but her voice was strong, determined. "That's kind of you, Mr. Jones, but we have to get the paper out."

"I'll help Jake." He tried to conceal the discouragement he felt, but didn't quite succeed. "There won't be much to print."

Her brown eyes probed his face. "Is something wrong?"

"Yes, I'm afraid there is. It's obvious the merchants are trying to force us out of business. They've withdrawn their ads again."

"I was afraid of that."

"It seems they have a nice little monopoly here in Maxwell, and they don't want anyone rocking their boat. When we, I, printed the miners' complaints, they concluded that I am the kind to do that."

"What're we gonna do, boss?" Mahoney had stepped closer.

"I have to say . . . if I were you I'd go to Leadville and find other employment. I'm told there are several

127

newspapers in Leadville."

"Do we have anything at all to print, Mr. Jones?"

"Some. Not much. Some of the news I do have concerns plans by a Denver merchant to build a general store here. And then of course . . ." Jones shook his head sadly. "There's news of Mr. Tucker's death. A little national news came in the mail. We have something to print, but not much."

"Mr. Jones." The brown eyes were locked onto his. "May I write the obituary for Mr. Tucker. He was my best friend, the best friend I ever had."

"Well." He couldn't look at her, and he could feel the disappointment she felt. He reached another decision. "Yes. I've been told that you are a literate woman, Miss Dubois and, after all, you knew Mr. Tucker better than anyone else. Yes, you write it and we'll print whatever you write."

"I'll get to work on it." She went to the back of the room, found a piece of newsprint and a pencil and, using a workbench for a desk, started writing.

"Now Jake," said Jones, "as soon as I look over the mail copy, you can start setting it. It won't take me long to write what little news I have, and when I finish I want you to show me how to set type."

"You're not gonna let 'em run you off?"

"Well, I can't say how long I can stay in business with the funds available, but I'm willing to gamble what little I have. When the new store moves in someone is going to have to advertise whether they like me or not. I only hope I can hold out that long."

He sat at his desk, took a pencil and began writing about the city council meeting: "The regular July meeting of the Maxwell city council was held Tuesday night for the transaction of general business. His Honor Mayor Wilbur Osgood occupied the chair . . ."

He finished the story, wrote a short letter to Nathaniel Martin of Denver, and had started reading the mail copy when the lawyer, Justus DeWolfe, came in.

"I've been advised that I might find Miss Dubois here," he said.

When she came forward, he offered his condolences. "Mr. Tucker was a fine gentleman, a real scholar. I admired him very much, and I know his passing is a terrible loss to you."

No one spoke, and he went on: "I have some information for you, Miss Dubois, that you probably are not aware of. Mr. Tucker didn't want it known until after his death. He left everything to you; his home, his horse and buggy, and his bank account, which amounts to, let's see . . ." The lawyer withdrew a paper from his coat pocket. "Five hundred and forty-two dollars."

Her eyes were wide and her mouth opened and closed without saying anything.

"He said to tell you . . ." DeWolfe looked at another paper and read from it. "He said to tell you that he has, had, no one else, and that you were the best friend he had in this world."

She covered her face with her hands, and her shoulders shook as she cried silently. Jones got up from his desk chair and gently guided her into it. He wanted to put his arms around her, but he didn't know whether that would be appropriate. He wanted to do something. He didn't know what to do.

Finally, he said, "Take the day off, Marybelle." He realized he had called her by her first name, and again he didn't know whether that was appropriate. "Take as much time as you want." Then he turned to Mahoney. "Jake, it's about time I learned how to do some of the physical work around here."

The lawyer bent over and spoke softly to Marybelle Dubois, then left. Jones went over to the type cases and frowned at them. He went from there to the flatbed chase and frowned again. "How in the world can you read this stuff backward?"

"You'll learn, boss."

Jones was trying to figure it out when the girl wiped her eyes with the palms of her hands and went back to her stool at the workbench.

"You don't have to do that, Miss Dubois."

"Naw, Marybelle," Mahoney added. "You just inherited enough spendoolicks that you don't have to work for a long time."

"Yes, I do," she said softly. "I do have to work."

At supper time, Jones remembered what Mahoney had said about socializing only with the town bigshots, and he realized that the printer had a point. The town fathers would tell him what they wanted printed in the newspaper and nothing else. The place to find out what was really going on was where the workingmen congregated. He went to the Ace Cafe for supper.

The same waiter wearing the same unwashed apron served him a bowl of venison stew and two thick slices of homemade bread. It was surprisingly good. "Nice evening," Jones said pleasantly, trying to make conversation.

"I dunno," the waiter replied sourly. "I been workin' in here all day."

Jones turned to the man in dirty clothes seated next to him at the counter. "I've often wondered what it's like to work below ground—in the mines. I don't think I'd care for it. You don't even know what the weather's like until the end of your, uh, shift."

"You get used to it." That was all the miner had to say.

After supper, Jones decided to go back to *The Times* and practice setting type. But on second thought, he stepped through the big pine door into the Deerfoot saloon. He hoped that by rubbing shoulders with the working men he'd pick up some news.

Instead, he got into the first fist fight he'd been in since his early teens.

Chapter Fifteen

The beer he ordered was warm and bitter, but he forced himself to take another swallow. It was the conversation between two men standing next to him at the bar that attracted his attention.

"Old Ben Tucker finally gave up the ghost, I hear," said a moustachioed man in bib overalls.

"Yeah, but I'm bettin' he died happy," said his companion, a man with a wild, bushy beard and a pillbox cap. "That breed gal that's been livin' with 'im could make a dead man get up and pee over the fence."

Jones felt anger rising within him. He knew his face was red, and his ears burned.

"Yup. I'm bettin' when she shucked that dress and crawled in the soogans with 'im he forgot about the consumption and ever'thing else."

"What did you say?" Jones turned to the bearded one and faced him, hands on hips.

"Who're you? What's it to you?"

Jones spat the words out. "Marybelle Dubois is a friend of mine."

"Yeah, well I'll tell you somethin', mister. She's half Injun, and I know them squaws. They'd take on a billy goat if somebody'd give 'em a bottle of whiskey."

The moustachioed man guffawed. "She's a looker,

but she's still a squaw."

"Haw-haw," went the bearded one. "I'd shore like to dip my wick in her lamp."

Jones wasn't hearing anymore. His eyes were fixed on the ugly mouth almost hidden inside the wild beard. It was repulsive, and it was spitting out hate, insults, venom. He didn't realize he was doing it, but his right hand was suddenly balled into a fist and it came up from somewhere around his middle, connecting solidly with the ugly mouth.

He felt the shock clear up to his shoulder, but it felt good and he followed the right hand punch with a left hand swing that caught the bearded one staggering backward. "Shut up," Jones hissed through his teeth. "Shut your filthy mouth."

The bearded man staggered back a few steps, stood there dazed, then shook his head and charged. He was four inches shorter than Jones but huskier, and when he bore in with large fists flailing, Jones felt his lips suddenly go numb and his vision become cloudy.

A fist connected with his chin, snapping his head back so hard it felt as though his neck had broken. Another fist slammed into his right eye again, and blood poured from a cut above the eye, shutting off half his vision.

Anger and frustration hurt him as much as the other man's fists, and he managed to keep his hands up and hit back. "You dirty, lying sonofabitch," he hissed, lashing out almost blindly.

His fury put some strength into his punches, and the bearded one was careless long enough for two blows to land solidly. Jones had the height and the reach, and somehow he made that work for him, punching

133

straight out, cursing as he punched.

The two stood toe to toe trading blows, hurting each other, until finally a hard right hand caught Jones in the mouth, staggering him back against the bar. He wanted to turn away, but there was nowhere to turn. His opponent saw victory then and swung big fists wildly.

For a moment, Jones could only cover his head with his arms, wishing the punishment would cease. Another blow hit him on top of the head and another on the arms. The bearded man was sure of victory now and moved in closer, so close that Jones could smell the stale beer on his breath.

Jones's legs wobbled and he almost fell. No, he told himself, I will not fall. I will not give in to this hateful, filthy sonofabitch. He straightened his legs, intending to pull himself up to his full height, but the man's face got in his way.

He felt a sharp pain on the top of his head as his opponent suddenly fell back, blood gushing from his nose and staggering weakly.

Jones willed himself to keep punching, and he swung his right fist and then his left and then his right. He could only see a blur but he kept swinging at it, and he could feel his punches connecting.

Then there was nothing in front of him, and he stumbled over something on the floor and went down on his knees. He wanted to stay there, but his mind wouldn't let him. Get up. Get up, you long, tall drink of water. Hey, how's the weather up there? That's what his friends and relatives used to say when they wanted to tease him. What's it look like on the other side of Harmon Hill, a classmate once asked. Straighten your shoulders, William. He stood, swaying drunkenly, ready to strike out at anything that got in front of him.

But there was nothing in front of him.

He staggered back against the bar and tried to steady his legs, to keep them from folding. His face was numb, his head hurt, and his ears were ringing. It wouldn't take much to push him over, he knew. Timber-r-r. That's what someone always yelled when he was a kid and was thrown down in a friendly wrestling match with other kids. It always got a laugh. Timber-r-r.

Not this time. Stand up. Straighten your shoulders, William.

"You better get out of here, mister," someone said. "You better haul your freight out'n here. Old Lou's meaner than a rattlesnake. He'll go home and get his scattergun." Jones couldn't see who was talking, but the voice was earnest, serious.

"You whupped 'im far and squar'," another voice added, "but you'd better git."

He wiped at his eyes with the palm of his right hand, and his vision cleared enough that he could see the bearded man on the floor, on his hands and knees, head down, not trying to get up. Blood from his nose had soaked his bushy beard and was dripping onto the floor.

"Go on back to the Wyatt Hotel or wherever you come from," the voice urged. "You whupped 'im."

Another voice said, "That's that editor feller, the one that gave the Bijou bosses their whatfor."

"Is that him?"

"That's him."

"Thought he did all his fightin' with words."

135

"Wal, I don't know who got the worst of it, but he's standin' and old Lou ain't."

Jones squinted through his one good eye and tried to see who was talking. His vision was muddled again, and the men around him all looked alike, just moving blurs. One of the blurs moved closer and loomed before him. "I'd buy you a drink but I don't think you can swaller right now. If you can walk, better make tracks."

He moved toward the door, where he thought the door was. The blurs moved back out of his way. He found the door, pushed it open and stepped outside.

The cool night air revived him somewhat, enough that he could walk a little steadier. He walked, turned a corner and headed toward his late uncle's house. His house. His ears were still ringing and his steps were unsteady, but he kept putting one foot in front of the other. Gradually, his vision was clearing, but it was still far from normal.

At home, he managed to pump some cold water into a tin basin and splash it over his face. That helped for awhile. But then the numbness began to wear off and the pain began. Good God, how his jaw hurt. It hurt to move it, to open his mouth. His swollen right eye was sore to the touch, and the top of his head hurt. The knuckles of his hands, when he held them up before his eyes, were skinned and bruised. Where was his hat? He made his way to the bedroom and lay down without undressing. After awhile he would get up and take off his shoes and clothes and get into bed. He'd feel better in the morning.

A loud banging on the door brought him to his feet again. He went unsteadily to the door, but was afraid to open it. No telling who or what was out there. "Who is it?" His voice wasn't as strong as he wanted it to be.

"Sheriff Schmitt. Open up."

He opened the door. Enough light from two lamps spilled out the door to illuminate Omar Schmitt's unfriendly face. "What is it, sheriff?"

"You're under arrest. I got a warrant right here." Schmitt showed him a sheet of paper. The deputy stood behind the sheriff.

"Under arrest? Me? What for?"

"For assault and battery, that's what for."

He couldn't believe it. Not even after the steel door clanged shut. Arrested. Locked up in jail. His mother would be horrified. Every bone in his body ached as he lay on the steel bunk, using his coat for a pillow. He wished his vision would clear completely and his ears would quit ringing so he could think. What the hell was he doing in jail?

Assault and battery, the sheriff had said. That meant the man named Lou had signed a complaint. That wasn't supposed to happen in the frontier towns. Hell, when he suggested complaining to the law about being horsewhipped he was advised against it. He'd be laughed at. When men had differences, they duked it out or shot it out.

Now here he was in jail for assault and battery.

As weary and sore as he was he didn't sleep much that night. The steel bunk had no mattress, and he could lie on it only for short periods of time. He spent most of the night sitting up. And he didn't touch the breakfast that was brought to him. He didn't even look at it. He did manage to walk a little, to pace back and forth in his cell like a caged animal. When the outer door clanged open, he whirled around, ready to tell the

137

sheriff what he thought of him. But he kept his mouth shut when he saw Justus DeWolfe follow the sheriff in. They stopped in front of his cell.

"You only get a few minutes," Omar Schmitt said, giving Jones a hard eye. "No monkey business." He left.

"Miss Dubois sent me," the lawyer said, standing in front of the cell door, not touching it. "I've been retained to represent you."

"Yeah. Well, when am I getting out of here." My God, how his jaw hurt.

"Later today, I hope."

"What do you mean, you hope? There's such a thing as bail, you know. Even here."

"I know, but only the municipal judge can set bail, and he's not in town."

"The mayor? He's the municipal judge, I hear. Isn't he the one who signed my arrest warrant?"

"Yes he is. But he left town early this morning for Leadville. He told his clerk he'd be back late this afternoon. As soon as he gets back I'll nail him and get him to set bond."

"He's the only one who can do it?"

"I'm afraid he is."

"How the hell did I get arrested, anyway? I thought men around here are expected to settle things with their fists."

The lawyer studied the floor a moment, then said, "This is very unusual. I did a little checking, and what I learned is very interesting."

"Well?" Jones was losing his patience.

"The man you fought with, Louis Eddman, signed a complaint, but I don't think it was entirely his idea. I

138

have learned that the deputy sheriff, Sam Courtney, talked him into it, and they tried to get the town marshal, Waller Vaughn, to get a warrant from the mayor, but Vaughn ridiculed them. He told Eddman that if he couldn't take care of himself in a fair fight to forget it."

"So they went to the sheriff."

"Yes. That's the size of it."

Jones walked in a circle, rubbing the sore spot on the top of his head, then turned back to the lawyer. "It's a conspiracy to shut down the newspaper. They've cut off their advertising and now they've got me locked up in jail. That damned deputy is part of the scheme somehow."

"Or he's following orders."

"Whose orders?"

The lawyer shrugged. "Who knows. It could have been anybody, but I'm betting it was one of the clique, you know, the bunch that runs this town."

"Sure. One of them heard about the fight and found a way to get me arrested. Well . . ." Jones walked in another circle. "They can't keep me locked up forever. When I get out of here I'm going to put out a newspaper, and they aren't going to like what I print."

Chapter Sixteen

But Will Jones didn't get out of jail. Not for four days. He spent the first day pacing back and forth, sitting on the bunk with his head in his hands and cursing. He remembered all the cuss words he had learned during bull sessions in the dormitory at Missouri U and used them all, plus a few he made up.

When supper was served in a tin plate, he tried to eat, but his jaw was so sore he couldn't chew it. At night he hollered that he wanted his lawyer. He yelled and cursed, hoping he would be heard in the sheriff's office, but no one came through the door. All he got was a "Shut yer face," from an inmate in the next cell. "Shut your tater trap," another inmate yelled. The night was long and the steel bunk was uncomfortable. Jones didn't sleep at all.

Justus DeWolfe showed up again next morning, but he started shaking his head negatively as soon as he stepped through the door. "The mayor's still not back. He was supposed to be back late yesterday, but his clerk said she hasn't seen him."

"Well hell, damn, shit."

The lawyer's face registered surprise at the language Will Jones was using, and for a second Jones almost apologized. But then he said, "There comes a time when it doesn't pay to be a gentleman."

"I don't blame you. I'd feel the same way."

"Well, when am I going to get the hell out of here?"

Again the lawyer shook his head. "I wish I could tell you. Seems they're going to let you out when they get good and ready."

"Can't you do anything."

"Well yes, but not immediately. I can go to Leadville and get a writ of habeas corpus from the district court judge. It would take a couple of days, however, and I'm hoping the mayor will be back before then."

"Shit." Jones sat on the bunk and put his head in his hands.

The prisoner in the next cell used a bucket for a toilet, and the smell permeated the entire cell block. It was sickening. Jones walked, cursed, walked.

He tried to eat the supper that was shoved under his cell door, but couldn't.

"Hey, pal." It was the prisoner in the next cell. "If you ain't gonna eat that, give 'er to me." Jones handed him the bread through the bars, but couldn't get the soup bowl through.

Justus DeWolfe was still shaking his head sadly next day.

"Aw shit. What the hell can we do? There must be something we can do."

"Do you want me to go to Leadville and get a writ? As I said, that will take a couple of days, and if the mayor gets back in the meantime, I won't be here to represent you."

"I don't know. I don't know what the hell's the best

thing to do. I just know that I want out of here."

"I don't know either, Mr. Jones. It's like flipping a coin. I don't know which is the best route to travel. You tell me what to do and I'll do it."

"What day is this?"

"Friday."

"Can you get to Leadville today in time to see the judge? And can you get back tomorrow?"

The lawyer pulled a watch out of his vest pocket. "I believe I can catch the stage if I hurry. Is that what you want me to do?"

"Do it."

Friday, he had said. On Saturday the paper was supposed to go to press. Jones sat on the bunk and stared at the floor. When he thought about the newspaper his depression deepened, and he let out a long groan and rolled over on his side.

There wouldn't be a paper this week.

It was late Saturday when he was released. "I just got back," Justus DeWolfe said as the sheriff unlocked the cell door. "I got to Leadville after the judge had gone home for the day, but I went to his home. He was madder than hell for being disturbed at home, but when I explained what was happened down here, he signed the writ."

Jones's legs were a little unsteady when he walked down the plank sidewalk. He had eaten and slept very little in the past four days and nights. Good God, what a mess I am, he thought. Thank God Mother can't see me. He fingered the scar on his cheek and the cut over his right eye. She'd cry all night if she could see this.

He wanted to go home and clean up, take a bath, shave off the four days' growth of brown beard, put on some clean clothes and find something to eat. But he had to see what was going on at the newspaper first.

What he saw surprised him. His two employees were hard at work rolling the press. Jacob Mahoney was pulling and pushing the flatbed chase under the rotating cylinder which laid newsprint down as it rotated and put enough pressure on it to make an inked impression. At the end of each pull, Marybelle Dubois cut off the paper and turned the cut sheets over so they could be printed on the other side. While she did that, Mahoney pushed the flatbed under the press again. After five runs, he had to pull a lever, raise the press and pour more ink into a series of small inking rollers.

They were so intent on their work that they didn't see him enter. Mahoney was the first to glance his way and spot him.

"Whup. You're back, boss."

Jones said nothing; only stared.

"We're gonna have to work late," Mahoney said, "but we're gittin' a paper out."

The girl came over and stood in front of him, a worry frown between her brown eyes. "Are you all right, Mr. Jones?"

He managed a lopsided grin. "I look like hell . . . pardon me . . . I look terrible, but I can still function. Would you tell me what in the world you're doing?"

"We're printing *The Maxwell Times*, and we'll have papers on the street by morning."

"But how, uh, what . . ." He didn't know exactly

143

what he wanted to ask.

"It was Marybelle that done it, boss. She done the writin' and editin', and we worked late a couple of nights, but we're gittin' 'er out."

"I hope you don't mind, Mr. Jones. We thought it important that publication not be interrupted."

"Mind? I, uh . . ." He went to a pile of freshly printed and folded newspapers, picked one up, looked at it, and started reading the lead story:

"Editor Jailed; Judge Leaves Town."

The headline was set in eighteen-point type, Jones had learned that much about printing. A subhead in twelve-point type read, "Plaintiff Also Leaves Town After Brawl In Deerfoot Saloon."

His eyebrows went up in spite of the cut over his right eye, and he read on:

"Times Editor William Jones was jailed Tuesday night on a charge of assault and battery following a brawl in the Deerfoot saloon.

"It was the first time such charges were brought in Maxwell County. Municipal Judge Wilbur Osgood, who is also Mayor of Maxwell, signed a warrant for Jones's arrest, then left town. As this newspaper goes to press, he still has not returned.

"Sheriff Omar Schmitt said Jones cannot be released on bond until Judge Osgood sets bond, and Jones must remain in jail until the judge returns.

"Complainant is Louis Eddman. He signed a complaint against Jones, claiming Jones assaulted him. Eddman was seen boarding the stage to Leadville the next day, and apparently hasn't been seen in Maxwell since.

"Attorney Justus DeWolfe told *The Times* that

Jones's arrest appears to be a conspiracy to stop publication of *The Times*. 'I'm probably sticking my neck out by saying this, but I think it's obvious,' DeWolfe said.

"Witnesses said a fistfight erupted between Jones and Eddman over some remark Eddman made. They said the fight was fair and no weapons were used.

"Town marshal, Waller Vaughn, told *The Times* that Eddman and deputy sheriff, Sam Courtney, went to him saying they wanted to sign a complaint, but he sent them away. 'I never heard of arresting a man for a common barroom brawl,' he said. 'If I arrested everybody who got in a fistfight I would have prisoners stacked up in the county jail like cordwood.'

"Jones's arrest came after the town merchants canceled their advertising in *The Times*. DeWolfe accused the merchants of trying to drive Jones out of business because he reported the employees' side in a story about two accidental deaths at the Bijou Mine.

"Readers will notice that there is no advertising in this issue, and also that the price per copy has gone up to five cents. We regret having to raise the price, but it is necessary to keep this newspaper in business without advertising."

Jones put the paper down and stared at Marybelle Dubois. "Did you write this?"

"Yes, Mr. Jones. I hope you don't mind. I thought the citizens should know."

For a moment, he could do nothing but stare in astonishment.

"I thought someone should do something. I realize I can't write as well as you, but . . ."

"It's, uh, all right. I have to think about this a

145

minute."

"I also edited some mail copy, Mr. Jones. I, we, wanted to get as much news as possible on four pages, and I edited out some of the words and sentences."

Jacob Mahoney moved over beside the girl, hands on his wide hips. "She done the best she could, boss. If you're gonna git mad at somebody git mad at me."

"Mad? Uh, whose idea was it to raise the price per copy?"

"Mine, boss." Mahoney kept his position. "Marybelle's not to blame for anything."

"Blame?" Suddenly he felt a weak, sickening ache in the pit of his stomach. "I owe you two a great deal. I . . ." His head was swimming and his legs were weak. He wanted to sit down.

"Mr. Jones, you should go home. Have you been eating? Mr. DeWolfe said you weren't eating. Let me cook something for you. I'll come back and finish my work here after you've eaten."

"Well, I, uh . . ." He tried to grin. "To tell the truth, I don't feel so good."

"Jake, help me, will you. Let's get him home and get some food into him."

"Shore. Here."

With his two employees supporting him by the arms, Will Jones walked unsteadily to his late uncle's house—his house. On the way he mumbled, "Mr. DeWolfe is right about a conspiracy to shut down the paper. But there's more to it than that. There's got to be a lot more than that."

Chapter Seventeen

Marybelle Dubois was back early next morning. He interrupted his shaving to answer her knock on the door. "I thought you'd like some fresh eggs and milk for breakfast," she said, waiting to be invited in. "I bought some from the widow Cuddigan."

He stepped back. "Please come in, Miss Dubois. Here, let me help you with that." He reached for the basket of groceries she carried.

Her smile showed those even white teeth again. "You're feeling better, aren't you? We were worried last night, and we hoped that all you needed was a good night's sleep on a soft bed and some good food."

Grinning, he said, "I think I'm going to live now." He closed the door behind her, went back to the water closet and finished shaving while she busied herself at the stove. While he finished dressing he kept the bedroom door closed between them and was dismayed when he saw the sorry condition of his shoes. He would have to buy some new shoes, some mountain hiking boots, perhaps.

Breakfast was the most tasty meal he had eaten since arriving in Maxwell. The eggs were fried exactly the way he wanted them—with the yokes a little runny—and the hot biscuits and molasses made him eat and eat until he felt stuffed. His jaw was still so sore that he couldn't chew the bacon, however.

"I should have known," she said apologetically.

"It's getting better." He grinned. "I'll be as good as new in a few days. I'm lucky I didn't lose some teeth."

Over his objections, she started washing the dishes and promised to meet him at the office as soon as she was finished. He got to the office ahead of her, but a few minutes behind Jacob Mahoney.

"Jake," he said, "I want you to know that whatever I said last night, about the work that you and Marybelle did, wasn't intended as criticism. Believe me, I'll never blame the two of you for anything. I'm deeply in your debt."

"You're aces with us, too, boss. Me and Marybelle, we're plannin' to hitch Ben Tucker's horse to the buggy and take some papers out to some minin' camps today. She ought to be here any minute."

"She will be. It'll be interesting to see whether they'll buy papers at five cents per copy."

"We figger it's a gamble, boss, but we figger it's time to ante up or git out."

"You're probably right."

The girl drove up in a horse-drawn buggy, and she and Mahoney loaded stacks of newspapers in the buggy and left. Jones prowled through the building alone, realizing that he was very fortunate, very fortunate indeed, to have such loyal employees.

Five cents per copy. That would be fifty dollars if they sold every copy. That would at least pay the bills. If they could do it, *The Times* would last.

Idly, he picked up a copy and sat at his desk and read. For over an hour he read. He put the paper down, gazed at the ceiling, then read some more.

Her sentences were short and simple, not the kind that would earn passing grades in the Missouri U. English Department. Still, they had a kind of—he tried to think of the right description—kind of simple charm. Charm? Well, not exactly, but—

For instance, take this paragraph that came in the mail from Denver:

"Authorities here admittedly continue to be baffled by the complete disappearance of nearly a ton of gold ingots which was stolen at gunpoint just outside the Denver mint at six-thirty o'clock on the evening of January 21, 1883, and they reluctantly admit that they have no clue to its whereabouts."

With Marybelle's rewriting, the paragraph read, "Authorities in Denver are still puzzled over the disappearance of nearly a ton of gold, stolen last Jan. 21.

"The gold ingots were taken at gunpoint just outside the Denver mint early in the evening."

Jones read the two versions again, and finally had to smile. She had managed to write exactly the same thing in fewer words, and she wrote it with more punch.

He read more of Marybelle's editing and read the original local stories she wrote. Finally, he had to chuckle. She didn't waste any words, that was certain. And, come to think of it, by not wasting words she was saving time. Time was money.

And her story about his arrest. She had done a thorough job. Instead of just going to the sheriff, she had interviewed witnesses to the fight, the town marshal, and the lawyer, Justus DeWolfe. And she told the story the way it ought to be told, without injecting her opinion.

"Maybe," Jones chuckled aloud, "maybe I ought to let her do the writing and editing while I set type."

But then, while he was going over everything in his mind, a worrisome thought returned. It came to him while he was in jail, and the more he thought about it the more it worried him.

Sure there was a conspiracy against him. But there had to be more than that. A little monopoly, such as the one the merchants had here, could be very profitable. No doubt many merchants made huge profits in the frontier towns. But it couldn't last forever. Sooner or later, unless the town died on its feet, someone would find a way to come in with another store, another restaurant, another drugs and sundries.

And even, Jones thought with a wry smile, another newspaper.

No, there was something else. Something much more important than a monopoly. But what?

It was Sunday and the government offices were all closed, and Jones didn't know what to do with himself. He wished he had gone with his two employees to deliver papers. He wondered if Justus DeWolfe was in his office. Probably not. He prowled the office and print shop, went back to his house and ate lunch, then came back and sat at his desk.

His two employees were all smiles when they returned. "We sold a lot of papers, boss. Ever' paper we left on the sidewalk in Maxwell is gone, and the cigar boxes are full of nickles and pennies. We didn't sell all

150

we took to the camps, but we sold a lot of 'em and I'm bettin' some folks'll buy the rest."

The girl handed him four cigar boxes full of coins. She chuckled. "The bank will have a conniption when they have to count all these pennies."

He grinned and said, "Let them have a fit. The important thing is we're still in business in spite of everything that has happened." He shook his head and laughed. "I'm surprised. I didn't think they'd pay a nickle."

"It was Marybelle's story, boss. Ever'body heard about you gittin' locked up, but they didn't know the whole story till they read it in *The Times*."

"You did a fine job of reporting, Miss Dubois," Jones said. "That's exactly what a newspaper should do: Tell the whole story. How in the world did you get Justus DeWolfe to say what he said?"

"He volunteered it. I didn't have to coax him. He said he had nothing to lose by making the town mad at him."

"He has complained about the lack of business for a lawyer in Maxwell, and he's planning to leave in the near future."

"He ought to go up to Leadville, boss. I hear there's so many lawyers up there you can't throw a stick across the street without hittin' two or three of 'em."

"That's why he came here. He's got the field to himself. Only the field is nearly empty."

They talked awhile, then the girl said she had to get the horse back to Mr. Tucker's stable and feed him. Jones put the coins in a canvas bag and went home.

That night Marybelle Dubois disappeared again.

151

"I don't know where she is, boss," Jacob Mahoney said next morning. "She's always been here by this time of day."

"Tell me how to get to Mr. Tucker's house, and I'll go over and see if she's there."

At the house, no one answered his knock on the door. He went around back and found the buggy, but the stable was empty.

"Aw, it's nothin to worry about, boss," Mahoney said when Jones told him what he had found. "She always goes somewhere on that horse ever' onct in a while. Most of the time she goes on Sundays, but we delivered papers yesterday so she went today."

"Where does she go?"

"DamfIknow. She never says. I always wondered, but I figgered it was none of my business."

"Well, she's certainly earned the day off." Jones gathered some copy paper, picked up a pencil and left.

He was surprised to find the mayor in his office. "Where were you?" he asked bluntly. He was convinced he had spent time in jail unnecessarily, and he knew the mayor was at least partly to blame.

"Now look here, Mr. Jones, I don't have to answer to you."

"Uh-huh," Jones aid, hooking his thumbs inside his belt. "Tell me this, Your Honor, when is my trial scheduled?"

The mayor swiveled his chair around and put his elbows on his desk, his back to Jones. "The charges have been dismissed."

"Oh? Why?"

"The plaintiff has decided not to press the case."
The mayor didn't look up.

"Did he tell you that?"

"Yes. Uh, no. That is, he can't be found. Without
a plaintiff we can't go to trial."

"I see. Tell me, whose idea was it to have me
arrested?"

The mayor looked up sharply then. "Whose idea?
You know very well whose idea."

"Was it yours? Or John Pope's? Or Oliver
Scarbro's?"

"Now see here, you had better be careful with your
accusations. And you had better advise your lawyer
friend to be careful, too. There are libel laws, you
know."

"Yeah, I know." Jones turned to go, then stopped.
"But the way I understand the law, truth is a pretty
good defense against libel. We can prove everything
that was printed in *The Times*."

Justus DeWolfe had his feet on his desk again and
kept them there when Jones entered his office and sat.
"They won't sue," he said. "I didn't just run off at the
mouth. I gave it some thought. They won't sue
because everyone in Maxwell County knows it's true,
and a jury wouldn't give them a penny."

"In a big city they might build a case against us,
isn't that right?"

"Yeah. But not here. They can't fool anyone here
for very long."

"And that brings up another point." Jones crossed
his long legs and studied his scuffed and torn shoes.
"I have a feeling, just a feeling, that something else is

153

afoot here. A bigger conspiracy of some kind. But I have no idea what."

DeWolfe pondered that. "I don't know. They've got a good thing going, and they're greedy enough to do most anything to keep it going. The last thing they want is a troublesome newspaper editor."

"But it can't last. Sooner or later someone will move in and put a stop to their monopoly."

"Sure, but by then they'll be able to retire rich."

"There's something more." Jones frowned at his shoe. "I wish I knew what it is."

Marybelle Dubois showed up next morning before *The Times* opened for business, before Jones had finished his breakfast.

"I apologize again for disturbing you this early," she said as she stood outside his front door, "but there's someone I think you'd like to meet."

"Meet? Who?"

"My grandfather. He's waiting for us up there." She pointed to the high, purple hills to the east.

"Your grandfather? Up there? What's this all about?"

Her brown eyes were round and serious. "Mr. Jones, it's about your uncle's death."

Chapter Eighteen

They were on their way by sunup on two bay horses rented from the Ardmore Livery. The girl said she had to leave her inherited horse at home to rest. Two miles out of town they quit the road and headed their horses up a steep narrow canyon trail.

The girl sat her horse easily, wearing a long dress with a billowy skirt which covered her and the saddle. Jones hadn't been on a horse for several years, and he felt uncomfortable. He also felt uncomfortable wearing a gun, the big Navy Colt that Jacob Mahoney had insisted he carry in a holster strapped around his waist.

They rode up the canyon on a trail that followed a creek through willows, around boulders, and over fallen timber. The canyon walls rose steep in places, and in other places there were pockets in the canyon where the green grass and wild flowers grew knee high. Tall ponderosas and the broad-leafed aspens grew in wide spots near the creek. The girl led the way silently, and Jones was grateful for that. He didn't want to talk. He was too intent on watching the horse he was riding, afraid it would stumble over a rock or something and fall on him. He didn't want a broken leg.

At the top of the canyon, they left the creek and crossed a wide valley covered with wild flowers of every color and shape. Here, there was no trail, but the girl seemed to know exactly where she was going.

His knees were so cramped they were screaming at him by the time they crossed the valley and entered the tall timber. There, the girl brought her horse to a stop.

"How are you doing, Mr. Jones?"

"Fine, I think. But I don't think I'll ever straighten my knees again."

She flashed a smile and dismounted. "Get off and stretch your legs. Maybe I can adjust your stirrups so your knees won't get so cramped."

He dismounted stiffly and walked slowly, stretching one leg at a time. The girl unlaced some leather thongs on the stirrup straps and lowered the stirrups on his saddle, then laced the thongs up again. "That should be more comfortable, Mr. Jones."

"Call me Will. That's what my friends call me."

The smile was back. "Certainly."

"How much farther, Miss Dubois, Marybelle?"

"We've reached our first destination, Will. I'd like you to meet my grandfather."

He jumped, startled, when he saw the man standing not more than twenty feet behind him. The man looked something like the pictures of Indians he had seen in the magazines. But not exactly. The pictures showed young Indian braves, standing tall, lean and straight. This one was old, short and bowlegged.

And this one didn't have a feathered headdress, but

156

instead had his thick white hair pulled back and tied in a knot behind his head. The clothes were familiar, however. Everything was made of leather, a light, supple leather.

The jacket with long sleeves and no collar, the pants with no fly in the front, and even the moccasins were made of the material. Buckskin? Jones assumed so. But there were no fancy fringes nor beads, and the leather was dark, nearly black, in the worn spots. The man's face was as round as a full moon, brown and covered with a million tiny wrinkles.

He made no move. Not knowing what else to do, Jones stepped toward him, holding out his hand. "How do you do, sir. I am William Jones."

With a snaggletoothed grin and a grunt, the Indian shook his hand once and let it drop. Jones turned to the girl. "Does he speak English?"

"No, Will, he speaks only Ute."

"Oh. What is his name?"

"It's uh, well, in English it's The Man Who Slaps Bears."

"You're joking. You're not joking."

She was still smiling. "No. When he was a young man he crept up behind a grizzly bear, just to show off to his friends, and slapped it on the rump and ran. If the bear had caught him it would have killed him."

Jones had nothing to say to that.

The girl and the old man talked with what sounded to Jones like a series of ya-yas, nyas, umps, oohs, and unhs. Finally, she turned to Jones. "He wants us to follow him."

"To where?"

"He wants to show you something. Something I

157

think you'll find very interesting." She got on her horse, arranged her long skirt over the saddle. He mounted, too, and discovered the lengthened stirrup leathers were more comfortable—while sitting still, that is. As soon as the horse moved, he missed the security of the shorter stirrups.

The old Indian took off on foot at a dog trot, and the horses had to strike a trot at times to keep up with him. Jones was amazed at how fast the old man could travel. His moccasined feet beat a steady rhythm.

The rough trotting gait made Jones's teeth rattle while the girl rode easily. Jones wondered if her horse had springs in its legs. Once when they slowed to a walk he managed to ask, "How long can he go on?"

"For hours, Will. He has always traveled on foot. In fact, he has never ridden a horse, wagon, or anything. Every place he has ever been in his life, he walked. Or ran. Except, of course, when he was a tiny baby."

"Amazing. Can he outdistance a horse?"

"Given enough time he can. A horse can outdistance him for two or three days, but when a horse gets tired it takes longer to recuperate. Grandfather can catch up with a horse in time."

On they went, over a pine-covered, rocky ridge, across a narrow valley, over another ridge, around a pile of huge boulders, across a creek, through a clump of willows so dense that Jones was afraid of being dragged off his horse. He wished the old man would stop so he could stop and get off the horse.

It was late afternoon when the Indian stood on top of a high ridge and pointed at something below. He stood with his arm straight out, forefinger extended. Jones got off his horse, walked up beside him and looked. All he saw was another narrow valley, which looked exactly like the other valleys they had crossed.

"What's he pointing at?"

"Down there, Will, is where your uncle died."

They descended the steep slope slowly, Jones leaning far back in his saddle to keep from sliding over the horse's head. The girl still rode easily, comfortably. At one point where his horse's forefeet dropped down from a two-foot-high ledge, Jones groaned, "Oh my God."

"Don't worry, Will. That horse won't fall."

He couldn't help letting out a sigh of relief when they finally reached the bottom and started across fairly level ground. The old man took off at his dog trot again, and the horses trotted a ways, walked a ways and trotted a ways to keep pace with him.

When finally they stopped, Jones dismounted painfully and had to hang onto the saddle horn a minute to keep his knees from buckling under him. The heavy gun pulled the gun belt low on his hips, and he had to hitch it back up. Grunting, the old Indian said something to Marybelle, and she said something back.

"Here's where it happened, Will."

Jones looked around. They were in a valley green with shrubs that looked like sagebrush, except that the bushes were covered with tiny yellow flowers. Granite rocks the size of a five-gallon can were scattered around, showing above the tall grass, as if a giant had rolled them out of his hand.

"How do you know?" he asked.

"It's clear to see. Look." She took four steps and squatted. He squatted beside her. "See the marks."

He could see nothing that resembled marks. "Where?"

"Right here." She put her forefinger to the ground. "Look closely. Afternoon showers have eroded the prints, but some of the marks are still here."

He looked closely. "Oh yeah, I see something." He looked around, trying to find more small depressions in the ground. "Is that a piece of a hoofprint?"

"Yes. There are many hoofprints. There were more than two horses."

"More than two? I was told that Uncle Nathan had two horses."

The girl turned to her grandfather and spoke again in that Umwa, nay, nya, oh, ump language. Her grandfather held up four fingers.

"Four?" Jones asked.

"Four. Mr. Benchley was not alone."

"Where did they come from?"

She asked her grandfather. He held up two fingers and pointed to the west, then closed his fist and held up two fingers again, this time pointing back the way they had come.

"Mr. Benchley came from the west and was joined here by two men who came the way we came."

Jones mulled that over. The old Indian squatted, dug up a double handful of dirt with his fingers, held it close to his mouth and gently blew on it.

"What in the world . . ."

"He's trying to determine how easily the soil here erodes in the wind and rain. That way he can tell us approximately how long ago these tracks were made."

"How long?"

She turned to her grandfather and relayed the

question, then got an answer. "Approximately . . . well, it was around forty days ago."

He nodded his head. "That figures. But then . . ." Jones frowned in puzzlement. "I was told that a search party followed Uncle Nathan's tracks back here. Wouldn't they have left tracks here, too?"

"They did. There were three of them. But the tracks left by Mr. Benchley and the two men who accosted him are a few days older."

"How can you tell that?"

"It's not difficult. We can tell by the weathering of the rocks that were disturbed by horses' hooves, by the ground where the rocks originally were, by the grass that the horses grazed when the men dismounted, by the age of the footprints, and by . . . well, try this. Take a pinch of dirt here where there never was a rock."

Jones took a pinch between his thumb and middle finger.

"Taste it."

He put it in his mouth and made a face at the gritty feel of it.

"Now taste this." She pointed to a depression near where a small stone was overturned.

Jones did as instructed.

"Is there a difference?"

"Yeah, I guess so. That last dirt I tasted seemed a little, uh, not quite as dry. Not moist either, but different."

"Keep in mind that that pinch of dirt had been covered for eons, while the first pinch has been exposed to the sun, the wind, the rain, and snow. Grandfather considered the amount of rain that has fallen, and by tasting and by close examination he has determined that this rock was turned over about five days earlier than that one there."

"That's amazing."

"There is more to be learned here, Will."

"What?"

Again she conversed with her grandfather. The old man pointed to two rocks, lying side by side near an assortment of other rocks, and spoke again.

"What did he say?"

"It's getting close to sundown. My grandfather's camp is near here, and we'd better spend the night there. My grandfather wants to show us more in the morning."

He looked at the sky. The sun was sitting on top of a high hill on the west. "Stay here?"

"Yes. We could go back in the dark. Horses have excellent night vision, and I'm sure these horses know the way home. But there is more to be learned here."

The thought of a long ride back didn't appeal to Jones, and he agreed. The girl mounted again and he followed, wincing as his buttocks came into contact with the saddle. Again it was trot a ways, walk a ways, trot. A mile farther they came to the old man's camp.

It consisted of a simple tent made by hanging a piece of canvas over a rope stretched between two trees. The canvas was pegged down on both sides, forming an A shape. The remains of a campfire were clearly visible in front of the tent, between it and a six-foot-high boulder. The old man had dug a small hole, filled it with cabbage-sized rocks and built his fire over the rocks. A small creek gurgled pleasantly near the camp.

Also clearly visible were a leather sack and a burlap bag hanging from a tree limb. Inside the tent a couple of blankets were spread on the ground. The blankets were wool and were obviously made by white men, and so were the large iron skillet and fire-blackened iron kettle.

The girl unsaddled her horse, led it to the creek to drink, then hobbled its front feet together with a pair of rawhide hobbles. Jones managed to unsaddle his horse, but couldn't figure out how the hobbles worked. She did it for him.

"I'm sorry, Marybelle. I'm a city man, you know."

She smiled, those white teeth gleaming. "I'd be as helpless as a baby in the city."

The horses were happily eating the tall mountain grass.

Which reminded Jones that he and the girl had had no lunch, and he wondered what they were going to eat. The old man answered that question without saying a word.

First he broke dead branches off the pine trees and whittled some shavings from one with a long-bladed knife. Then he reached into the leather bag and produced a small bow with a loosely fitted leather thong for a bowstring, a sharp stick and a small rock with an indentation worn in the center of it. He wound the bowstring once around the stick, put the sharp end of the stick point down against a block of wood, piled his shavings around it, held his stone on top of the stick, and started sawing on the bow.

As he sawed, the stick spun first one way and then the other, and soon the friction brought a small spiral of smoke from the block of wood. The old man kept

163

on sawing until the shavings caught fire. He knelt until his face was only inches from the shavings and blew gently. The fire grew. With his bare hands he scooped up the burning shavings and deposited them on the rocks in his fire hole. Then he piled more sticks on top of that.

When he had a good fire going he reached inside a burlap bag and produced a sack of cornmeal.

And suddenly a mystery that had been pulling at the back of Jones's mind was solved.

He grinned at the girl. "Now I know where you've been disappearing to every Sunday."

She returned the smile. "You're right."

"But why?"

She sat cross-legged on the ground, her long dress covering her from neck to ankles. He wondered what she wore under her dress, and guessed she was wearing some kind of pantaloons or pantalettes.

"He's a runaway, Will. He's an Uncompahgre Ute, and he was raised in these mountains. When the soldiers herded the Utes into a reservation down south, he ran away. Oh, he doesn't mind the reservation so much in the winter, but in the summer he comes back here. If the authorities knew they would take him back to the reservation." She chuckled. "That is, if they could catch him."

Jones chuckled with her. "Unless they could recruit the eagles to scout for them, they'd never find him."

"I bring him some white man's groceries so he doesn't have to hunt meat very much. He's old and entitled to his comforts."

"Does he stay right here?"

"Oh no, he moves around. I always know approximately where he is, and when I want to see him I just ride around until he finds me."

"Does he call to you, or something?"

"Oh yes. I recognize his call. He can imitate an eagle's screech, or a coyote's howl, or a raven's raucous call, or just about any other creature, and the white men don't know the difference. He raised me so I do know the difference. And sometimes he just appears in front of me."

"He's an amazing tracker. I wouldn't have seen a sign of anything human if you hadn't pointed it out to me. And then I saw very little."

"Indians learn tracking at a very early age. While the white kids are playing their games, Indian kids are playing tracking games. Studying the ground gets to be a habit. You'd be surprised at what you can learn from the ground."

"Like how my uncle died?"

"Yes. It's very clear."

"Tell me about it."

"I'll tell you this much tonight, Will, and tomorrow we'll prove it to you. Mr. Benchley was murdered."

Chapter Nineteen

Using the heated rocks as a stove, the Indian boiled some water in the pot, then added corn meal until he had a soft dough. While the water was heating, he heated some beef tallow in the skillet, and when the dough was ready, he dropped it, a glob at a time, into the hot grease. With a long-handled spoon, he flattened the globs of dough into cakes and, lifting them out, he placed them on a heated rock.

When he had a half-dozen cakes ready to eat, he poured the grease out of the skillet into a small crock and poured in a can of beans.

They ate with their hands after spreading the beans on the flat corn cakes and rolling them up. It was surprisingly good, but Jones couldn't chew the pemmican which the Indian brought out of his leather bag.

The girl explained to her grandfather that Jones had a sore jaw, and the old man nodded his understanding. He poured the grease back into the skillet and made more corn cakes, which Jones ate until his stomach was full.

They slept in their clothes. The girl and her grandfather shared a blanket inside the tent, and Jones slept outside wrapped in another blanket close to the fire. He had read about cowboys using their saddles for a pillow, and he turned his rented saddle upside down and cradled his head inside the sheepskin-lined skirts. It smelled of horse sweat. Twice during the night the Indian got up quietly and put more wood on the fire. Jones shivered in the cold mountain air at times, but most of the time he was warm. He had to take the gun belt off, though. He just couldn't get comfortable with it strapped around his waist.

Breakfast was more corn cakes and some canned peaches, which they ate out of the cans. Toilet was the creek and the privacy of some boulders on the other side of the creek.

The old Indian rolled up his blankets, took down the tent and rolled it up.

"He'll move camp when we get back," the girl explained. "He doesn't like to stay in one spot too long."

"Where are we going?"

She pointed to a long pine-studded ridge that paralleled the valley they were in. "Up there. Then we'll come back here, and from here we'll go back to town."

They rode to the top of the ridge, the old man leading the way on foot. On top, they walked their horses slowly while their leader studied the ground. Suddenly, he stopped and pointed to something at his feet.

What he pointed at was easy to see. It was a cigarette butt and a burned wooden match. The cigarette butt had been ground into the dirt, obviously by a boot heel, and had been there for some time.

"Someone was up here," Jones said. "Does it mean something?"

"Wait," the girl answered. "There's more."

Her grandfather took off again at a fast walk, eyes to the ground. He stopped again, and Jones and the girl dismounted.

"You can see the tracks yourself, Will."

He bent over and finally saw some small indentations in the ground and a spot where half a hoofprint was visible. Puzzled, he looked up at the girl. "I still don't know what this means."

"Look there." She pointed.

What Jones finally saw was the imprint of something. He didn't know what. And when he looked carefully he saw more small, shapeless indentations.

"And here."

He saw nothing out of the ordinary where she was pointing now. "What is it?"

"See how the ground has been smoothed out right here, where the small rocks have been pushed aside, where the grass has been flattened and is not quite back to its normal shape."

"Well, yeah, I guess so."

"A man sat here. He got off his horse and sat here on the ground. Look at the grass behind you."

Jones looked, still puzzled.

"The top of the grass has been grazed off. The man sat here a long time, long enough for his horse to crop all this grass."

"Oh." That was all Jones could say.

The girl's grandfather was traveling again, and they followed, this time walking and leading their horses.

168

A quarter mile farther they stopped again. Now the signs were easy to see. There were the blackened remains of a campfire and a discarded tin can.

"He, whoever he was, stayed here for the night," Jones said.

"Yes, and Grandfather said he spent five nights camping in different spots along this ridge. There was only one horse and one man. Look,"

She pointed to a pile of horse manure. "Grandfather believes it was left here while your uncle crawled on his hands and knees down there."

The Indian had again dug up a double handful of dirt and was blowing on it. When he dropped it he looked at the girl and nodded.

"There's no doubt. These tracks were made the same time as those tracks down there."

A sudden sick feeling came over Jones as the realization hit him. "Oh my God."

"Now you know," the girl said matter-of-factly.

He looked at her, his features pulled tight in mental anguish. "How could he? How could he sit up here and watch Uncle Nathan try desperately to crawl for help?"

"He wanted Mr. Benchley to die."

All Jones could do was sit on the ground with his head in his hands.

"We can show you more. We can show you where the man spent four other nights, all within sight of the valley down there."

He could only groan and shake his head sadly.

"Mr. Jones." She stood beside him and put a hand on his shoulder. "Do you care to see the rest?"

"No." He looked up at her again with a pained

expression. "I don't need to see any more."

"There is one more thing I think you should see."

"What?"

"Let's go back to where it all started." She mounted and Jones followed.

With the old man leading the way again, they rode down off the ridge and went back up the valley to the spot where the girl said Nathan Benchley had suffered his broken leg. The two large rocks which Jones had noticed before were still there. The riders dismounted.

They watched the old Indian pick up one of the rock, look at its underside, blow on it, then point to a small depression in the ground. The girl explained to Jones.

"First, that stone was picked up by a man. You can see where it sat before it was picked up. Second, it was used to pound something. If you look close enough you can see a spot of gray on the underside where it came into contact with something. By blowing on it Grandfather removed any dust that might have accumulated since then and uncovered the marks."

"I'm almost afraid to guess what it came into contact with."

She waited for him to figure it out.

"But I can't believe . . . wouldn't Uncle Nathan have put up a struggle? He wouldn't have just sat there with his right leg across that rock and let someone pound on it with another rock."

"He was unconscious, knocked out."

"How do you know?"

"It's easy to see. This is rocky country, and nothing can walk over the small rocks without disturbing them. A rock that has been in the same spot for thousands of years can't be disturbed without leaving a mark. Look." She squatted and pointed to a stone the size and shape of a man's thumb. "Someone stepped on this one, and though it didn't turn over it moved half an inch. See?"

He saw, by studying it, that it had indeed been moved a fraction of an inch from its original position.

"Over there." She was pointing to more rocks. "The marks on the ground are still discernible, but the stones tell the story more clearly. Mr. Benchley was dragged from here to that large rock. Someone had his arms around his chest, and dragged him backward. The signs are parallel. And the heel marks here." She put her forefinger on a small indentation in the ground near a clump of grass. "The man's heel dug in here. He was walking backward, dragging something."

Jones groaned again. "Oh my God. And when Uncle Nathan regained consciousness he had a broken leg and his horses had run off."

She nodded affirmatively.

"And he tried for five days to crawl to a road where he hoped someone would come along and help him. And . . ." Another long groan. "While he was doing that, someone stayed up there on that hill and watched him. Why?"

"To be sure he died. Just in case he did manage, by some miracle, to reach help, the man up there was supposed to shoot him. That's my guess."

That sick feeling washed over Jones again, and for a moment he feared he was going to vomit. He managed to swallow the bile in his throat and finally managed to speak in a strained voice, "It was murder.

171

It was murder made to look like an accident. It was an extremely cruel murder."

He walked away slowly, head down, trying to rid himself of the sickness that had spread from his stomach into his chest. He walked. No one followed. He groaned and walked. He sat on a rock and hugged his knees. Finally, he stood and walked back. His voice quavered with anger when he spoke.

"Two men accosted him, hit him over the head and knocked him out, then deliberately broke his leg, chased his horses away and left him to die. One stayed behind, got up there on that hill and kept an eye on him just to be sure he died. Is that the way you see it?"

Marybelle Dubois talked to her grandfather in Ute, then to Jones. "He agrees. That's the way it happened." Her eyes softened. "I'm sorry, Will. If I had been here . . . if I hadn't gone back to the reservation, I might have been able to find him. Save him. With Grandfather's help I know I could. I'm so sorry."

Jones was still full of anger, and his lips twisted. "That man up there would have shot him and you, too." He grimaced with anger. "Somehow . . . somehow I've got to find out who did it and see them hung."

Chapter Twenty

No one spoke for a long moment, then the girl and her grandfather talked in low tones and separated, the girl going to her horse and the old Indian going at his dog trot back toward his camp.

"Will you tell your grandfather something for me? Will you give him my thanks. I've never met anyone like him. I really admire him."

"He understands. He likes you, too."

"But why? I haven't done anything to earn his respect."

"I like you, and that's reason enough for him."

Jones felt the anger draining out of him as he watched the old man going away. "I sure hope to meet him again some time."

"We can get back to town before dark if we start now," she said.

It was a painful ride back for Jones, and he thought it would never end. Twice the girl paused to point out something she thought interesting: a porcupine scurrying along, bristling with sharp needles, unable to move fast, a coyote that was following them but keeping a good distance between them. When they passed a twelve-foot-deep hole in the ground with fractured rocks piled around it, she said simply, "Prospector's hole." •

"What? Oh, a hole dug by someone looking for gold or silver?"

Once, when they crossed a grassy valley they could hear ravens making the most racket that Jones ever heard. There were a dozen or more of them flying back and forth past a ponderosa, caw-cawing in raucous tones.

"I'll bet they've got an owl cornered in that tree," the girl said. "Ravens hate owls. Let's go over and see."

She was right. The owl sat perched on a limb while ravens flew past it, clawing at it as they passed. The owl tried to escape by flying away, but the ravens harrassed it in midair until it landed on another limb in another tree.

"The owl has better weapons," the girl explained, "but the ravens can fly better."

"Darnedest thing I ever saw." For a moment Jones forgot about his weary, sore body and watched in fascination. "Can they hurt him?"

"No. They'll tease and torment him until dark and then he'll get away." She chuckled. "He won't come back here."

"You like the mountains, don't you, Marybelle."

"I love them. I was raised in the mountains."

"They're beautiful and really interesting. But I've read about men dying in the mountains, starving or freezing or being killed by wild animals."

She glanced at him and smiled a quick smile. "Mother nature can be very cruel, but if you learn to live with her, be a part of her, she won't hurt you."

"You're fortunate, Marybelle, to have been raised in the mountains and to understand nature."

"I wouldn't trade my childhood for anybody's."

"Still, you managed to get an education."

"My mother . . . even Chief Ouray . . . realized after the San Juan Cession ten years ago that the Indian lands were shrinking and there was no future for the young people there. They were right. Now my family—what's left of my family—is confined to a reservation down south. I'm lucky, I guess, that I'm half white, and I'm sometimes accepted by whites. When I was sixteen my mother took me to Leadville where we met Mrs. Hansen, and Mrs. Hansen took me to Maxwell. She was kind to me and taught me how to clean house and cook white man's food. She gave me time off to go to Mr. Tucker's school, and Mr. Tucker was also very kind to me."

"It took some ambition and determination on your part."

"I like to learn, and Mr. Tucker became a sort of private tutor."

"The way I heard it you repaid his kindness with some kindness of your own."

She shook her head sadly. "I could never repay Mr. Tucker." Having said that, her lips tightened and she looked away. Jones said no more, but he was silently glad that he had gotten in a few good licks at the man who insulted Marybelle Dubois.

They were about three miles away from Maxwell when two riders showed up on a rocky hill ahead of them. The girl reined up sharply, eyes narrowed.

"Who are they, Marybelle?"

"It's Sheriff Schmitt and his deputy."

"How can you tell from so far away?"

"I can tell."

"They surely won't bother us."

"I don't trust them, Will."

"You don't? Why?"

Without taking her eyes off the two riders, she said, "That deputy was one of the vigilantes, we know that. And there's something about Sheriff Schmitt that I don't like. He was too happy about getting to lock you up in jail and he kept you in jail as long as he possibly could. We can't trust him."

"Well, they've seen us and they're coming this way."

"Yes, and coming at a gallop."

"They want to talk to us about something."

"Will, I . . ." Her face twitched nervously. "They're heavily armed with pistols and rifles."

"Lawmen are supposed to be armed."

"I think we should get back to town as fast as we can. We can't go down the canyon trail. They'd cut us off. We'll have to take a longer route."

Jones pondered what she had said. "Tell you what. Why don't you go on and I'll wait for them. I'd like to know what they want."

"They could be dangerous."

"No, not if you get to town safely. They won't dare harm me because they'll know you recognized them and can testify against them."

"All right. You're the boss. But be careful." She

reined her horse downhill and kicked it into a gallop.

Jones's mount wanted to go with her, but he was able to hold it back. The two horsemen galloped uphill toward him, then suddenly one split off and went after the girl.

"Oh no you don't," Jones muttered. He slacked up on the reins, and his horse took off at a run, following Marybelle's horse. Jones had to hang onto the saddle horn to keep from falling off as the horse jumped gullies and dodged boulders, but he let it run as hard as it wanted to. It was a losing race.

The deputy below had the angle and was going to head the girl off before she could get much farther. His horse was fresh while hers was tired. He was going to catch her.

"No, by God, you're not," Jones muttered. He hauled back on the reins and got his mount stopped. He dismounted, forgetting the pain in his knees, and knelt on the ground. "Now," he muttered, "is the time to use this damn gun I've been lugging around."

He held the gun in both hands and cocked the hammer back. Without taking careful aim, he squeezed the trigger.

The explosion almost knocked the gun from his hands, and he knew his shot hadn't even come close to the man below. But the man brought his horse to a stop and looked uphill at Jones.

"If I were a marksman I could shoot him off his horse," Jones muttered. "Maybe I fooled him. Maybe he thinks I can shoot."

The deputy stared at Jones a moment, then touched spurs to his horse and again went after the girl. Jones fired another shot. That one must have

177

come close because the deputy stopped again.

"I'm getting better," Jones muttered. "Make one more move toward her and I'll shoot a hole in you."

The deputy turned his horse around.

The sound of hoofbeats behind him brought Jones around, too, and he saw Sheriff Schmitt bearing down on him, pistol drawn. Feeling desperate, Jones looked for a way to escape. His horse had shied at the gunshots and was standing on a bridle rein a hundred yards away. The deputy was coming uphill at him, and the sheriff was coming from behind.

Jones waited, the gun in his hand.

"Drop that gun," the sheriff yelled as he pulled up. "Drop it right now."

Jones let the gun slip from his fingers.

"Now." The sheriff brought his horse to a standstill. "Just what the humped-up hell do you think you're doin'?"

"What I did, sheriff, was keep that deputy of yours from bothering Miss Dubois."

The deputy rode up then, his horse blowing from the run. "That sombitch damn near shot me, Omar." He had his pistol pointed at Jones's chest. "I oughta fill him full of forty-five slugs."

"No," Schmitt said, "that breed girl saw us and she can identify us."

"Well, hell, are we gonna just let this eastern sombitch shoot at us and get by with it?"

"I didn't intend to hit you," Jones said, "just keep you from catching Miss Dubois." He turned to the sheriff. "Why in hell were you trying to catch her?"

"We was lookin' for you. We knew you left town early yesterday mornin', and we thought you might of got lost."

"You know better than that. You know Miss Dubois doesn't get lost."

"Weel . . ." Schmitt groped for words. "Old Pete at the livery wants his horses back."

"We told him we might be gone two days. He has no cause for worry about his horses."

"Weel . . ." The sheriff's face hardened and his eyes narrowed. "What we're doin' is none of your business. You're lucky I don't arrest you for shootin' at an officer of the law."

"No jury would convict me. Not after Miss Dubois tells how your deputy chased her."

"I could keep you in jail for a long time before a trial can get started."

"No you won't. You pulled that kind of shit once and you, by God, won't do it again."

The sheriff and the deputy looked at each other, and finally the sheriff shrugged and holstered his gun. "Git the hell out of here."

Jones picked up the gun he had dropped and went to his horse.

It was dark when Jones rode into the canyon. He couldn't see the trail, but he remembered Marybelle saying horses could see in the dark. He hung onto the saddle horn and let the animal pick its way. The horse wasted no steps, and soon they were on the road to Maxwell. The girl was waiting at the livery barn, holding a lighted lantern.

"I was worried."

"I'm fine, Marybelle. Just a little tired. I'm not

used to riding."

"Did they give you any trouble? I heard the shots and saw the deputy stop chasing me."

"Naw. They were damned—darned—unhappy about those shots, but they decided not to do anything about it."

He unsaddled his horse and followed her lantern into the barn. She had already put hay and water in a box stall, and he turned the horse loose in the stall.

"What do you suppose they were doing up there, Marybelle?"

"I have no idea. Did they give any kind of explanation?"

"Yeah, they said they were looking for us. They thought we might be lost. I don't believe that. Do you?"

"Not for a minute."

"I wonder what they were doing." He couldn't see her face in the dark. "Is there any chance that they meant us harm?"

"I don't trust them, but . . . I just don't know."

"Well, if there's any possibility at all that someone wants to harm us, you'd better not stay alone in Mr. Tucker's house."

"I won't. I'll stay at the Hansen House. Mrs. Hansen will find a place for me to sleep. You'd better be careful, too."

"Don't worry about me. I can lock both doors, and I've still got Jake's gun."

He walked with her to the Hansen House, then went back to his own bungalow. He was bone tired and sore, and his mind was weary, too. The mental picture of his uncle, the way he had died, the way he had tried desperately to survive, wouldn't leave his mind.

Why did it take so long to get a search party organized? And why did it take so long to find him? Who all was involved in Uncle Nathan's murder?

Chapter Twenty-one

Marybelle and Jacob Mahoney beat him to the office next morning. She was wearing a clean dress and had her hair brushed until it shined. Her "good morning" was cheerful and helped bring him out of his cloud of gloom.

"We'll be working late, Will, but we'll put out a newspaper this week."

"I'll help set type," Jones said. "I'll probably never be as fast at it as you two, but I can help a little. First, however, we have to have something to print."

He opened the mail that had arrived by stage the day before and went through the mail copy, picking out what he thought might be of interest to the citizens of Maxwell County. That done, he grabbed a sheaf of copy paper and a pencil and went out on the street.

His first stop was the sheriff's office, and he found the sheriff and his deputy both there. They glared at him but said nothing until he asked, "How many men in jail today?"

"Why?" the sheriff asked.

"It's public business."

"Two."

"What are the charges against them?"

"Charges? There ain't no charges."

"Why are they being held?"

Reluctantly, the sheriff told him. One man was arrested for shootin another man in the foot, and one was arrested for butchering a calf that didn't belong to him. "He was caught red-handed," Schmitt said.

Jones got all the information he needed there and went next to the mayor's office. The mayor wasn't in. "Oh, by the way," Jones said to the mayor's clerk, "where is the town marshal's office?"

He went to the marshal's one-room log cabin on Coulter Street and found the door locked. He started to leave when he saw the marshal walking toward him. Marshal Waller Vaughn was tall, buggy whip lean, with a hawk nose and a clean-shaven face. His gun belt and holster were dark with age, and the gun butt that protruded from the holster was of hand-carved walnut.

"Lookin' for somebody, Mr. Editor?"

"Yes, Mr. Vaughn, I thought it was time I met you. As a news reporter and editor, I should have gotten acquainted with you sooner."

"Well, you're meetin' me." The marshal's voice was businesslike but not unpleasant.

"I heard, that is I read, about how you refused to arrest me for fighting. I want to thank you."

"If you'd shot somebody or used a knife, I'd've grabbed you so quick it'd made you goggle-eyed. But I can't arrest everybody that gets in a fistfight."

"Not even when someone signs a complaint?"

"Oh, I reckon if the mayor signed a warrant I'd have to, but when they came to me they didn't have a warrant yet. They must of got that later."

Waller Vaughn opened the door to his log-cabin office and went inside. Jones followed. Wanted posters decorated a wall, and a lever action rifle with an octagonal barrel stood in a corner.

"Marshal, you know just about everything that goes on in town, don't you?"

"Well." Vaughn pushed his high-crown hat back, uncovering a shock of iron-gray hair. "Just about."

"Can you think of any reason my uncle, Nathan Benchley, was murdered?"

"Murdered?" The marshal dropped into a wooden chair and looked hard at Jones.

"Yes, murdered. I'm convinced of that, and I'd give anything to find out who did it and why."

"See here, Mr. Editor, everything I've heard about old Benchley's death sounds like an accident. He ain't the first to go up there and not come back alive. Men get lost up there, get hurt, get crippled and can't get back." He squinted closer at Jones. "What makes you think he was murdered?"

Jones didn't answer immediately. He wondered whether he should tell about the old Indian and all the signs that pointed to murder. He decided this was not the time or place to do it. Finally, he said, "It's just that some strange things have been going on. You know, don't you, that the businessmen tried to force my uncle out of business? Have you any idea why?"

"All I know is old Benchley was part of their little bunch till he wanted me and Omar Schmitt to do some sleuthin' about Bertrum Hansen's wreck."

"He did? Did you investigate?"

"Naw. Trouble was, he didn't come to me with his suspicions till a month after the wreck, and then he

184

didn't know nothin'."

"He had to have had a reason for being suspicious."

"Well yeah, at least he thought he did. He said John Pope tried to buy the Maggie Mine from Hansen and Hansen wouldn't sell, but after Hansen was killed John Pope and Oliver Scarbro bought it from his widow."

"Did you know that?"

"Well, I heard talk about it, but that don't prove nothin'."

"The way I understand it, an ore wagon turned over on him even though the wheels were chain locked. Is that what you understand?"

"Yeah, I heard talk. The wheels were locked with an old log chain that was bolted together in a couple of places. It came apart, and the wagon slid sideways and turned over. The skinner, a man named Wylie, jumped off the other side. The wheel horses were jerked down but the lead team kept on pullin'. They pulled the wheel team back on their feet and dragged the wagon on its side for about fifteen yards before the pin twisted out of the doubletree. Hansen was under it."

"Was there anything about the wreck that made you suspect . . . that could have indicated foul play?"

"Naw. Nothin'."

"Did you say my uncle went to the sheriff, too?"

"Yeah, he did, and Omar couldn't find anything suspicious."

Jones mulled that over, then with rancor, he said, "But what the sheriff did do was trot right over to his big-shot friends and tell them what Nathan Benchley said. They realized then that my uncle had a suspicious nature and could become a troublemaker, and they decided to discourage him from doing business in Maxwell. Is that the way you see it?"

Waller Vaughn seemed to be trying to look right through Jones. Then he lifted his shoulders in a shrug. "Talk about a suspicious nature, you lead the parade, son."

"Yeah." Jones was sarcastic. "I'm getting suspicious as hell." He was silent a moment, then asked, "Was the Maggie Mine a good one?"

The marshal shook his head. "Far as I know. Old Hansen took a lot of good ore out of her. Built that big Hansen House, the biggest house in town, and had money in the bank."

"It's a gold mine, isn't it?"

"Yeah, just like John Pope's Bijou Mine. They're both among the richest goin' anywhere."

Jones thought that over, but couldn't find anything significant in it. He asked about news, got none and left.

He wrote what little news he had and again tried his hand at setting type. At noon he was persuaded to go to the Hansen House for lunch, and he was glad he did. Lunch was chicken stew with potatoe dumplings, homemade bread, and apple butter. He was ashamed of the way he stuffed himself.

Sitting at the long table, elbow to elbow with laboring men, seemed strange at first, but he was pleasantly surprised at how well mannered they were. And it was obvious that they had just washed their faces and combed their hair. Their hair was plastered

186

down with water.

"Please pass the bread," the man on his left said. Jones did, and asked for another helping of stew. It was passed from hand to hand until it got to him. The men were served by two women, one young and the other middle-aged, both wearing clean white aprons. Mrs. Hansen sat at the end of the table.

Conversation was light while the men ate, but one man in bib overalls asked Jones when the new store was coming to town. Jones had to admit he didn't know.

After lunch, Jones and his two employees worked in the shop, setting type. They worked until seven-fifteen, then Jones and Jake Mahoney went back to the Hansen House for supper. Marybelle Dubois went to the house willed to her by Benjamin Tucker. She had to care for the horse, she said. Later they met again in the shop and worked until ten o'clock when Jones looked at his watch and said, "Enough. It's way past time to quit for the day."

"Another day like this one, boss, and we'll get the paper out on Saturday night like always."

"Yeah," said Jones. "We could use more local news, though."

Next morning he had more news.

Chapter Twenty-two

It was Jacob Mahoney who told him about it. The printer was both worried and excited. "Marybelle done escaped by the skin of her teeth, boss."

"Escaped? Where?"

"It happened at Ben Tucker's house, or I guess it's her house now. She was in bed when she heard somebody breakin' in."

"What?" Jones could feel his heart beating faster. "Where is she? Is she all right?"

"Yeah, she's all right, but scared. She was so scared when she pounded on the door at the Hansen House last night she was almost as white as you."

"Where is she?"

"She'll be here in a minute. She had to go feed her horse."

She came in then, looking tired but clean and neat with a red ribbon tied around her dark hair and forehead.

"What happened, Marybelle?" Jones couldn't hide the fear and worry he felt.

"It was . . . well, let me begin at the beginning. I was in bed when I heard a noise at the back door. I went in my barefeet in the dark to see what it was. I could hear someone trying to unlock the door. At first I thought I'd slip out the front door, but when I went to the front door I heard someone walking on the porch. It's a wooden porch, you know." She paused.

"Yeah? What happened?"

"I put my shoes on and a robe and slipped out a window in the living room and ran to the Hansen House."

"And you went back there just now?"

"Yes, I had to take care of the horse. The back door was broken in. The doorjamb was broken. It looks as though someone just hit it with his shoulder until it broke. Nothing else was disturbed."

"Have you reported this to the sheriff?"

"Not yet. Mrs. Hansen is going with me to the sheriff's office. She'll be here in a few minutes."

"I'm going, too."

Sheriff Omar Schmitt was outraged. "I'll find out who done it, Miss Doobwah, and I'll bring him to justice, you can bet your boots on that."

"There was more than one."

"Oh yeah, you said you heard someone on the front porch, too."

"Sheriff," Mrs. Hansen said, "what do you suppose they were after?"

Schmitt hitched his gun belt around and drawled, "Weel, if nothin' is missin', then I reckon they wanted to, uh, take advantage of a young woman alone." His

189

face grew hard. "Men are hung for things like that around here."

"How," Jones asked, "do you go about solving a crime of this kind?"

"Weel, I'll go look at the house. See if I can find anything that might be a clue, then me and Sam'll ask a lot of questions of a lot of people. Somebody might of seen somethin', or heard somethin'."

"Is the town marshal going to be involved?"

"I'm the top law officer in Maxwell County, but if Waller Vaughn wants to help, he'll be welcome."

On the way back to *The Times*, Jones asked Marybelle why she had been spending the night alone. "I thought you were going to stay at the Hansen House."

"Mr. Tucker's house is my house now. I'm either going to live in it or sell it. I'd rather live in it."

Jones wrote the story: "A young woman was rudely awakened Wednesday night by intruders who broke into her home in Maxwell only to find that she had heard them breaking in and had fled.

"Miss Marybelle Dubois related that she heard strange noises at her back door, and when she investigated she determined that someone was trying to unlock the door. Miss Dubois went next to her front door, hoping to escape by that route, but heard footsteps on her front porch.

"The young lady foiled the intruders, however, by slipping out a window and running to the Hansen House where she spent the remainder of the night.

"Her house was the home of the late Benjamin

Tucker who died only last week. In his will he left all his property to Miss Dubois, and she has set up permanent residence there."

Jones wrote on, trying to keep his sentences less complex and his paragraphs shorter. When he finished he read it carefully, wondering whether he had written in the best style and whether Marybelle Dubois could write the story better. He had to admit, reluctantly, that she quite possibly could.

The three of them worked until ten o'clock again that night, and Jones got Marybelle to promise to spend the night at the Hansen House.

"You ought to be careful, too, Will. Whoever wanted to harm me might pick on you next."

"Do you think, then, that your knowledge of my uncle's murder might somehow be connected with what happened to you last night?"

"I don't know. It's possible."

"Yeah, boss. You keep that old hogleg of mine for awhile. Keep 'er loaded and handy."

"I will. I certainly will."

It was on his mind when he blew out the lamps and went to bed. For a long time he lay awake, fearful that every noise he heard was an intruder with homicidal intentions. He had Jacob Mahoney's big pistol fully loaded and lying on a table within reach of his bed.

Dammit, he said to himself, I feel like a child afraid of the dark, afraid to sleep alone. Dammit all anyway.

He realized suddenly that his bed was next to a window, and that made him feel more vulnerable. No one could break the window without waking him up, but he still felt uneasy.

He got up, pulled the mattress from the bed and carried it to the living room, away from any window. He put the pistol on the floor beside him, covered himself with some blankets and finally went to sleep.

Three hours later the whole world exploded.

Chapter Twenty-three

The explosion bounced Jones out from under his blankets and onto his feet.

"What the hell? What the holy hell?"

He stood there in his nightshirt, trying to gather his senses around him, trying to figure out what happened.

His mind spun like a top, throwing out questions but no answers. Did something explode? What? Where did the noise come from?

He picked up the Navy Colt, cocked the hammer back and tiptoed to the kitchen door. It was still intact. Holding the gun waist high, ready to fire, he made his way barefoot to the front door. No damage there.

It wasn't until he went into the bedroom that he began to see what had happened. The window over his bed had a hole in it the size of a baseball. Carefully, with the pistol ready, Jones looked through the window. He could see the dark shape of the ponderosas outside, but he saw nothing that moved.

He struck a wooden match and started to light a lamp, then quickly blew it out when it occurred to him that he was a perfect target standing there with a light in his hand.

Still, he wanted to see, to find out what happened.

After another long look through the bedroom window, Jones went to the living room and looked through the windows there, then the kitchen. He saw nothing suspicious.

Quickly he lighted a lamp, set it on the table beside the bed and stepped back away from it. Standing in a dark corner of the room, he saw the damage.

The bed springs looked as though they had been hit in the middle with a sledge hammer, and the floor under the bed had a splintered hole in it that Jones could put his fist through.

"Oh my God," he groaned when the realization came to him. Someone had fired a shotgun at the middle of the bed thinking he was in it. Someone had tried to kill him.

Jones blew out the lamp, went into the living room and sat on a short sofa in the dark. He still held the pistol. "First," he said out loud, "it was Marybelle they tried to kill and now me. If they keep trying they'll succeed. Sooner or later our luck will run out." He realized he was talking to himself, and he shut his mouth. But he couldn't stop his mind from spinning.

What can we do? Leave town? That would be the smart thing to do. That's probably what they want. They? Who are they? The town fathers, the clique, as Justus DeWolfe once called them? He couldn't be sure, and he couldn't make accusations until he was sure.

How can a guy defend himself? Carrying a gun doesn't help. They can shoot from ambush, from the dark.

What to do? Think. He turned it over in his mind, worried about it, and finally came to a conclusion. The only way they could defend themselves was to identify the enemy and stop them. That was the only way.

For the rest of the night Jones went over everything he had learned since he arrived in Maxwell, everything he had heard and everything he had seen. He read again in his mind the letter that Justus DeWolfe had mailed to his mother, telling about Uncle Nathan's death.

He forced himself to concentrate, to go over every detail again—and again. By first light, a vague thought began to germinate. At first he dismissed it, but it persisted until finally he allowed it to remain. Like a flower slowly blossoming, it grew.

It wasn't anything he had seen, nor was it anything he had heard. It was something he had read.

"I have to take the stage to Leadville," he told his employees. "There's something I want to check out."

"What is it, boss?"

"It's just something I read in *The Times*, a story that Marybelle edited. I want to know more about it. Since we have no back issues here, I'm hoping I can find earlier stories on that subject in one of the Leadville papers.

"Mr. Jones—Will—do you have an idea about who is responsible for what's happened?"

"I've got a weak theory, that's all. It's pretty weak right now, but it's the only theory I can think of. I won't be back until tomorrow. I'm sorry to leave you with so much work to do, but I've just got to check this out."

He put on his coat, looked for his fedora hat and remembered he had lost it in a saloon brawl. "Marybelle, don't go anywhere or do anything by yourself. Jake, you go with her. Here, take your gun and keep it ready."

"I'll do 'er, boss."

"Be careful, Will."

It had been only a month or so since Will Jones had seen a big city, but still he felt like a country bumpkin when he got out of the stagecoach and wandered onto Leadville's main street. Traffic on the street was so thick that wagons barely had room to pass each other, and foot traffic on the sidewalks was shoulder to shoulder.

A blanket of noxious black and yellow smoke hung over the city, and Jones could see that it came from five or six tall smokestacks surrounding the city. Mining and smelting seemed to be the big industries. A train whistle split the air, and more black smoke belched out of a locomotive's diamond-shaped stack.

He stopped a man on the sidewalk and asked the way to the *Leadville Times-Republican*. It was right across the street in a two-story brick building, a building that was built tightly against other brick buildings.

Inside, he asked for the editor, and a short, round, bald man wearing a green eyeshade was pointed out to him.

"Pardon me, sir," Jones said.

The editor looked up from his desk, a question on his face. Jones introduced himself, and the editor's face registered interest. "Oh yeah? I heard about Nathan Benchley's death, and I heard that a nephew of his from back East was taking over the paper."

Jones looked around the room. A dozen people were bent over desks writing furiously. "Is this a daily paper?"

"Yeah. One of a half dozen in Leadville."

"A half dozen?"

"Yeah, we're a big city now. We've got sixty physicians and surgeons in Leadville, and lawyers climbing all over each other."

Jones explained that all back issues of *The Maxwell Times* had been stolen and asked if he could see some back issues of the *Times-Republican*. He needed to look at papers printed from January twenty-first to the present, he said.

"Yeah." The editor pointed to another room with a glass door. "Help yourself, but don't get them out of chronological order."

Jones promised he wouldn't.

He quickly found what he was looking for. The story was printed on January twenty-third, and it had a Denver dateline. It told of an armed robbery just outside the Denver mint. Four men armed with shotguns overpowered five guards and made off with a team and wagon. The wagon was carrying a ton of gold ingots.

The five guards were bound hand and foot and left helpless in an alley where they stayed for more than an hour before they were discovered. A massive manhunt turned up the team and wagon but the gold was missing.

Jones looked through later issues of the *Times-Republican* and found several follow-up stories, but they contained nothing new. The identities of the robbers were still unknown, and the gold was still missing.

And, according to a story from Denver edited by Marybelle Dubois, it hadn't been found yet.

Jones thanked the editor and, out of curiosity, asked what kind of press the paper had. It was a Walter rotary press, he was told, and it would soon be for sale.

"For sale?"

"Yeah. We're shutting down next week. Too damn many newspapers, and old man Haney is shutting her down."

"Haney?"

"Yeah, he owns the Haney smelter and a general store, and he doesn't give a damn about this newspaper. It was something he started so he could lay his political views on the population, but it never did catch on."

"That's too bad. Wish I could buy it. The press, I mean."

"It'd be a good deal. I hear you're still printing with a flatbed press."

"Yes we are, and it's slow and tiresome."

"You ought to buy our press. It isn't the very latest, but it's better than what you've got."

"Wish I could."

On the street again, Jones went back to the stage and freight company, found out that his stage left early next morning, then hunted up a hotel. He was tired from the lack of sleep, and in spite of the awful street noise, he slept well.

Next morning the heavy black smoke still covered the city and burned his eyes.

"It's the weather," the stage driver said as he loaded luggage into the boot at the back of the coach.

"The weather?"

"Yup. You can forecast the weather by that smoke. If it's goin' straight up, the weather's gonna stay good, but if it's sliding down around the buildings, a squall's comin'."

He was right. An hour out of Leadville, the sky opened up and dumped water by the barrelsful on the coach, the horses, and everything in sight. The four passengers let down the leather window shades and kept dry. Lightning zigzagged across the sky and thunder split the sky open.

"Won't last long," a fellow passenger said. "These high-country storms don't last long."

It was a four-hour trip to Maxwell, and the stage stopped every ten miles to change horses. "It's an easy run to Maxwell," someone commented. "It's mostly downhill. Comin' back they have to let the horses slow down to a walk on the steep hills."

The two printers were hard at work when Jones got back to his office. He shucked his coat, rolled up his sleeves and went to work beside them.

"Find out anything, boss?"

"I learned something. I don't know whether it's significant."

199

Marybelle Dubois looked at him curiously.

They went to the Hansen House for supper, and after supper Jones went with Marybelle to feed the horse that Benjamin Tucker had left her.

"Marybelle," Jones said as they walked back to the newspaper in the darkness, "do you remember a story from Denver you edited last week about a robbery at the Denver mint?"

"Yes."

"Do you remember whether *The Times* had a story on that subject before my uncle disappeared?"

She thought about it a moment. "Yes, there was one story. It was in the last issue that Mr. Benchley edited."

"What did the story say?"

"Oh, just that the mystery hadn't been solved."

"There was nothing earlier than that? In January or February?"

"No, but Mr. Benchley didn't subscribe to the mail news until a few weeks before his death. It was after the merchants quit advertising. He said something about having to have something to offer the readers."

"Did you . . . would you know whether any more stories on that subject came in the mail after my uncle disappeared?"

"No. I never opened his mail."

"Uh-huh. And I take it then that when someone broke into his desk and stole all his papers the mail was stolen, too."

She stopped suddenly, took him by the arm and turned him toward her. "That's important, isn't it? You're thinking there's some connection between the robbery in Denver and Mr. Benchley's murder." Her

200

brown eyes were locked onto his and wouldn't let go.

"Aw." He shrugged. "I don't know. It's just a wild guess. I really have no information that ties the two events together."

"But you think it's a possibility." Her gaze didn't waver.

"It's an interesting thought." Again he shrugged. "It's hard to believe a robbery in Denver had anything to do with a newspaper publisher's murder in Maxwell County."

Her eyes continued to hold his, and her hand was still on his arm. He was very much aware of that, of her closeness, of her female softness. Her brown eyes suddenly turned away. A frown wrinkle appeared between them.

"I can't imagine how the two could be related, but it's something to think about."

"Yeah." They were standing close on a deserted back street in the darkness. "Yeah, you, uh . . ." What would she do, he wondered, if he suddenly put his arms around her and pulled her tight. "You, uh, won't mention this to anyone, will you?"

"Of course not. I never mention the newspaper's business to anybody."

"Sure. I know that. I . . ." What he did next, he did without thinking. If he had thought about it he wouldn't have done it. He moved a half step closer, put his hands on her shoulders, bent down and kissed her quickly on the lips.

She gasped and stepped back, her mouth open in surprise.

"I'm sorry. I didn't mean . . . I . . . please forgive me, Marybelle."

201

"Mr. Jones." Her tone was scolding.

"I really didn't mean to do that, Marybelle. I've never done anything like that before."

She stared at him, frowning.

"I promise I won't do that again. I promise."

Slowly, the frown vanished. A corner of her mouth turned up briefly. "Mr. Jones—Will." She spoke quietly. "Don't be so hasty with your promises." With that, she spun on her heels and took off in a rapid walk to the office of The Maxwell Times.

Chapter Twenty-four

Both Jones and Jacob Mahoney walked Marybelle Dubois back to the Hansen House at ten o'clock, then Jones went home alone, carrying Mahoney's big Navy Colt. He walked around his house before going inside, and once inside he walked through the rooms in the dark before he lighted a lamp.

Even then he lighted only one lamp and stayed away from it while he made his bed on the living room floor, next to the front door. He chuckled to himself when he realized he had developed a strong sense of self-preservation, something he had never needed before.

At his office next morning he edited some of the copy that had come in the mail and picked up his sheaf of notepaper and a pencil and started out the door.

The bearded man approaching him wore rough wool pants, a tight belt, and a floppy hat. He carried a cigar box. "Mr. Editor? Here. I just come in from Bluebird Crik and I thought I'd bring you your money."

"Money?" Jones was puzzled.

"Yeah, we bought all your papers, and this here's the money."

"Really?"

"Yeah. At first we borried papers from each other, then we decided that wasn't fair and we paid for all of 'em."

"Well . . ." Jones stuck out his hand. "I'm Will Jones."

"Cogswell. Joseph Cogswell."

"Mr. Cogswell, I certainly want to thank you. I didn't expect you to do this."

"We heered about the town honchos givin' you trouble, and we shore don't want to cheat you out of anything."

"I sure do appreciate this."

"It's nothin'."

"How are you folks doing out there on, uh, Bluebird Creek?"

"We're findin' some of that yaller stuff and some silver, too. We finally built our own mill, a half-assed one."

"Why did you do that?"

"Wal, the Bijou smelter won't take our rocks no more, and it costs too much to haul 'er to Leadville, so we built our own horse-powered stamp mill. It misses some of the good stuff, but it's still cheaper than haulin' ore."

"Stamp mill? Excuse my ignorance, Mr. Cogswell, but what is a stamp mill?"

The sidewalk where they stood was picking up traffic, and they had to step aside twice to allow pedestrians to pass. Finally, they stood to one side against the front of *The Times* building. Joseph

Cogswell hitched up his baggy wool pants, tilted his floppy hat back and tried to explain.

"Wal, you see, we built this big iron box, about eight feet squar, and we built this big sheet of iron so it fits inside the box. It's sort of like a ramrod, and we got 'er weighted to about two ton. We raise 'er up on a pulley with a team of horses hitched to a cable, then when she's at the top we lock 'er there and fill the box with rocks."

"Oh, I see. Then you let the ramrod drop and it crushes the ore in the box."

"Keereck. It usually takes several drops, but it smashes 'er up pretty good."

"Then what do you do?"

"We built a long tom. We take the smashed ore and wash 'er down this thirty-five-foot box over a bunch of riffles. We got 'er rigged up so we can shake the box and shuffle the smashed rock over the riffles."

"Um. I take it then that the lighter materials are washed aside while the heavier metals are trapped somehow below the riffles."

"Keereck. We got some mercury to help finish the job."

"But you said this is not the most efficient method, not as efficient as smelting?"

"Keereck. We miss some stuff, but what can you do?" The miner shrugged.

"And you said the Bijou won't process your ore anymore? When did they stop doing that?"

"About the first of March, when they bought the Maggie Mine. Old Pope said he couldn't handle any more than what he's bringin' out of the Bijou and the Maggie. He's only got one furnace."

"Then another smelter would probably be a profitable venture in Maxwell County."

"You betcha. But it costs money to build one."

"Um. Mr. Cogswell, I'd like to buy you a drink. I feel that I ought to repay you for your honesty and your information. I've learned things from you."

"Thanks, Mr. Editor. My old woman is over to the store buyin' some flour and stuff, and she's prob'ly waitin' fer me. You don't owe us anything. But I'll be glad to take a drink with you some other time."

"Any time, Mr. Cogswell. I'll be honored." Jones watched the miner walk away, his heavy boots clomping on the plank walk.

Jones shook his head in disbelief. The frontier West is a rough, tough place, he said to himself, and a man's life isn't worth much. But there are a lot of fine, honest, decent people on the frontier, too. They are the people who keep society alive, not the lawyers, judges, and politicians. And they, by God, were the people his newspaper was going to serve.

Will Jones apologized to Maggie Hansen for showing up uninvited in the middle of the afternoon. He explained that he was trying to learn more about the mining and smelting industry, and since her late husband was a mining engineer she might be able to help him.

"Why certainly, Mr. Jones." She led the way into a drawing room, closed the sliding doors, and invited him to sit on a velvet sofa.

Her brown hair was hanging in waves to her shoulders. A very attractive woman, Jones thought. But a little too old for him. And besides, as attractive as she was, she couldn't hold a candle to Marybelle Dubois.

Still, what a catch she would be for a middle-aged gentleman.

"Mrs. Hansen, I was wondering whether . . . uh, obviously the Maggie Mine was a profitable one. Your husband has apparently left you well off. But I was wondering just how profitable."

"She's a good mine, Mr. Jones. Bertrum knew exactly what he was doing when he filed his claim and built a hoist and started taking ore out of her."

"Did he have his ore processed at the Bijou Smelter and Reduction Works?"

"Yes, he did. He paid Mr. Pope by the ton."

"I see. Then John Pope and his employees processed his ore and turned the valuable results over to him?"

"Yes, that was the way they did business."

"Did? He doesn't do it that way anymore?"

"No. Now that he owns the Maggie, too, he has stopped taking ore from the other mines."

"Where does he sell the valuable metals?"

"It goes to Denver, where it is placed on the market. Brokers buy most of it, but the U.S. Mint buys some, too."

"Um. Well, with all that valuable gold and whatever being transported from one place to another it must be highly tempting to some of the, uh, criminal element."

"It is. But it is well guarded by men with rifles and shotguns."

"Oh? John Pope hires armed guards, then?"

"He has a half dozen. Most of them live in company houses, but one, Mr. Jackson, lives here. He's not married and he doesn't like to cook."

"Do you suppose he would tell me about his work? About how the gold is guarded, I mean?"

"He will if I ask him to. Of course, he did make it clear one day that he wouldn't under any circumstances reveal when the gold was to be shipped. Apparently that is one of the precautionary measures, not letting it be known when the gold is to be moved. That way, no one can plan a robbery."

Thomas Jackson, when Jones was introduced to him, would reveal very little—at first. "I'd be out of a job tomorrow, Mr. Jones. And believe me, totin' a rifle is a better job than muckin' in somebody's mine."

"Of course. I understand, and I apologize."

They were seated in the drawing room where Maggie Hansen had invited them before supper. Jones stood and started to excuse himself.

"All I can say, Mr. Jones, is it's well guarded. It'd take the army to get at it."

"Oh?" Jones turned back. "I suppose then that when the gold is processed, melted or whatever you do to it, it's well guarded until it is shipped."

"You bet. They pour it into ingots and keep it in a steel shed with a padlock as big as a man's hat. We take turns guardin' it day and night. But I'll tell you this much, Mr. Jones. They don't keep much of it around. We take it to Leadville and put it on a train as soon as we get a few of those bricks."

"Oh, I see. You don't accumulate enough at one time to make it worthwhile for a gang of criminals to go to the trouble and risk of trying a robbery."

"Right you are. But . . ." Thomas Jackson's face

clouded for a moment. "Lately we've been haulin' more than we used to."

Jones's eyebrows went up. "Is that right? Since when?"

"Since old Pope bought the Maggie Mine."

"Wouldn't that explain it?"

"No. He always milled rocks from the Maggie. We figger the Maggie's payin' off about double what she used to."

Jones glanced at Mrs. Hansen. She wore a puzzled frown. "Then," Jones said, "the Maggie turned out to be a very good investment."

"Ever'thing old Pope touches is a good investment. His Bijou Mine is gettin' richer all the time, too."

"Um. I see." That, Jones decided, was definitely something to think about.

Carrying a gun and taking precautions had become a habit with Jones now, but it was a habit he didn't like. Whoever wanted him and Miss Dubois dead wouldn't give up. He and the girl knew now that his uncle was murdered, and whoever was responsible wanted that bit of intelligence to go no further.

Uncle Nathan was killed because he knew something. Or they were afraid he would learn something. How could he have learned something that was a threat to anyone? The answer to that was simple, come to think of it. By editing a newspaper he was privy to information that most people were not. Every newspaperman in the world learned things they couldn't print. First, they had to have proof, and then there was the fear of lawsuits. And if it was a police matter, they couldn't print everything they knew because it might hamper a police investigation or tip off the suspects. Newspapermen could have some strong suspicions that they couldn't print.

Is that what brought on his uncle's murder? It had to be.

Chapter Twenty-five

"Marybelle," Jones said, "you are acquainted, aren't you, with some of the men who work in the Maggie or the Bijou mines? I mean, you got acquainted with them at the Hansen House, didn't you?"

"Of course. I know several miners. Why?"

"Well, I was wondering . . ." Jones sat at his desk, and Marybelle sat in the barrel chair. "I hear that John Pope is taking more gold out of those mines than should be expected. I was wondering what his mine employees think of that. Is it true?"

Her dark hair had a sheen on it this morning, and her skin was fresh and clear. Jones watched her brown eyes as they half closed while she was thinking. He never got tired of looking at her eyes. "Will," she said, looking up and locking onto his gaze, "this has something to do with Mr. Benchley's murder, doesn't it? And it has to do with that gold robbery in Denver."

He had to smile. "Yes. It's a sort of shot in the dark, but yes, there is a possible connection."

"What you're thinking, Will, is . . ." She paused. "What you're thinking is that some of the gold coming out of the smelter might have come from somewhere other than the mines."

His smile widened. "What do you think, Marybelle?"

Again her eyes half closed for a long moment, and again she looked up and locked onto his gaze. "It's as you said. It's a shot in the dark, but it's something we have to check out. Somehow."

Jones chuckled. "You didn't learn your English entirely from a scholar, did you?"

"What? Oh, no. Well, in a way, yes. Mr. Tucker liked colloquial English, and he was facinated by slang and regional dialects. He had notebooks full of it. And also, I learned a lot of my English by listening to conversations at the Hansen House."

"They taught you well, Marybelle. You learned well." He forced the smile off his face and forced his mind back to the mystery that had to be solved. "I guess the best place to start is with the miners. You can communicate with them better than I can, and it would be interesting to know what they think about the quality of ore coming out of the mines."

"I'll ask."

Ask she did. At the supper table that evening, with Jones sitting beside her, she somehow turned the conversation around to the subject she wanted to explore. Jones didn't talk—just listened.

"She's a rich 'un," a miner said between bites of boiled beef. "She's as good a vein as I ever did see, an' I've been a hard rock miner for nigh on twenty years."

"Has it gotten richer in the past few months?"

"Wal . . ." The miner hesitated. "Can't say she has. Don't seem like it to me, nohow. How about you, Hiram?"

"There's a vein down there about a hunnerd and fifty feet that ain't quit yet," Hiram answered. He wiped a spot of gravy off his beard with a linen napkin before saying more. "But she can't last forever. We're alookin' for another vein, goin' down to two hunnerd feet now, and shootin' rounds under Bijou Hill."

"Then there's no reason for Mr. Pope to be shipping more gold now than he has in the past?"

"Can't say for shore," Hiram answered. "Don't seem like it to me either."

"Old Pope's mighty lucky we don't hit water down there," another miner added. "Good thing we ain't blastin' into that there fault, or whatever they call it. Pumpin' water out gets darned expensive."

The conversation then turned to the problem of water in the mines, how expensive it was to pump it out and how miners often suffered serious illnesses from working in damp, cool places.

"Do you think we learned anything significant?" Marybelle asked while she and Jones walked to her house and stable.

"I don't know. I guess all we learned is it's possible that John Pope is shipping more gold than he's taking out of the mines. But we haven't proven it."

"And where would it come from, Will?"

He stopped and grinned. "Give you one guess."

"From the robbery at Denver. That's what you're thinking, isn't it?"

"You have to admit it's an interesting possibility. But it leaves a lot of questions unanswered."

"Uh-huh. Such as how did Mr. Pope get his hands on it."

"Somehow I don't take him for an armed robber."

"No. He's the gentleman type of crook. That is," she added quickly, "if he is a crook."

"Right. We can't accuse him yet."

"And what can we do if we find some real evidence that points to him?"

"That's another question we have to find an answer for."

They walked on. He helped her pitch hay to the horse and rake the corral. "I need to ride him more," she said. "It's not good for a horse to stand in a pen all the time."

"Aren't you going to the mountains to visit your grandfather anymore?"

"Not now. He's on his way back to the reservation. I took him all the groceries he could carry, and I only hope it's enough."

"He's leaving already?"

"He'll walk every step of the way, and it's a long way. He'll take his time and enjoy himself, and try to get back just ahead of the first deep snow."

Jones shook his head in disbelief. "He's a remarkable man. He just might be the only one of his kind in the whole world. I'd sure like to meet him again."

"Stick around, Will. He'll be back next summer."

"I'm planning to. Although, I hear the winters around here are long and severe."

"Winter isn't bad if you're prepared for it. We have plenty of firewood, and the cattlemen are more than happy to sell a side of beef, or the whole beef. Meat will stay frozen all winter. And I'm fortunate enough to have a neighbor who milks two jersey cows. He sells me all the milk and butter I need. The roads are seldom snowed in, and we have a lot of sunny, balmy days here in the winter so the snow doesn't stay deep very long."

Jones silently wondered what it would be like to spend a winter in the Rocky Mountains. Maybe, if he had someone like Marybelle to share a house with, it wouldn't be so bad. And a bed.

My God, he thought, here I am standing here thinking like that again. I've got to stop that. She's a very smart girl, and she might read my mind. "It's getting dark, Marybelle, and we'd better get you back to the Hansen House."

"Yes, Will."

Walking back to his own house alone in the dark he couldn't stop thinking about her. She was everything a man needed in a woman. Pretty. Smart. As honest and loyal as the day is long. Hard working. The kind that would do anything for a friend. And a husband.

But what would his mother and his aunts and uncles think if he went back to Kansas City with a half-breed Indian girl for a bride?

Because he was thinking about Marybelle Dubois he didn't see the man step out from behind a ponderosa and speak:

"Just stop right there, Mr. Editor." The man loomed up in the dark no more than eight feet from Jones. "Stop and stand still or I'll blow your guts out."

Jones stopped, squinted, trying to see the man's face in the blackness. Another man came from somewhere behind him. "Don't move, you sonofabitch." A pair of hands grabbed his arms and pulled them behind him.

"Who are you?" Jones's voice was high with sudden fear. "What do you want?"

A sneer came from the man in front of him. "You know who I am. Not that it matters a damned bit."

"Louis Eddman?" Jones thought he recognized the voice, but he wasn't sure.

"You guessed good, Mr. Editor."

The gun was taken from the holster at his hip, and his hands were tied behind his back with a rough hemp rope. "What . . . what are you doing?"

"You'll find out."

"You can't get away with this."

A cruel chuckle. "Hell we can't."

"Too many people know my uncle was murdered. Your feeble attempt at making it look like an accident didn't work. You can't do that to me."

"It ain't gonna look like no accident, Mr. Editor. You're gonna just disappear."

"Come on." The man behind him pulled on his tied hands and almost pulled him off his feet.

Jones was pulled backward and kept off balance so he couldn't turn around. "What are you going to do? You can't get away with this." He realized he was pleading, and he tried to put some dignity into his voice. "You'll be found out and prosecuted."

"Huh," one of them said. "They'll have to go a long way to prosecute us. The arm of the law they got around here don't reach that far."

"You can't go far enough. Too many people know about you."

"Huh?" The pulling suddenly ceased. "Who

216

knows about us?"

"Aw shit, he's just blubberin'. Nobody knows nothin' about us."

The pulling resumed. "S'pose they do know?"

"Well, even if somebody did know about us, we'd be better off with him dead and gone."

He was pulled backward fifty yards, and he heard a horse snort and stamp its feet. He still couldn't make out the men's faces.

"Damn, it's darker than a skunk's ass. Where'n hell is that damned buggy?"

"Here. Right here."

He was spun around and shoved up against the wheel of a buggy. "Git in."

"Light that lantern, will you? I can't find my ass with both hands."

"We don't want nobody to see nothin'. But we gotta have some light. I'll strike a match."

A match flared, and Jones saw the bearded face of Louis Eddman, the nasty face he had tried to pound into a bleeding mess. "Git your skinny ass in there." He was pushed up against a wheel of the buggy.

"Why? Why should I?"

" 'Cause I'll shoot your head off right here if you don't."

"Knock 'im in the head if you want to, but don't shoot 'im yet."

"I ain't gonna lift 'im in. He'll git in or I'll stick 'im with this knife."

He felt a sharp pain in his right side and knew a knife had punctured his skin. He groped with his left foot for the steel step, and with his hands behind his back, climbed awkwardly into the buggy.

"You got the lines? I'll untie the horses."

"I got 'em. How in hell're we gonna find our way?"

"I know the way. It ain't far."

"Where are we going?" Jones could still feel the pain in his side, and it added to the fear, making his heart race.

"You'll find out. It's the last thing you'll ever know."

Chapter Twenty-six

They were going to kill him. They had tried to kill him by shooting through his bedroom window, and when that failed they had formulated another plan. He suspected they would try again, and he stupidly walked right into their trap. How could he be so careless?

Blaming himself didn't lessen the fear, and his veins felt as if ice water were flowing through them. The second man climbed into the buggy, and Jones was between them. His wrists hurt where the hemp dug into his skin. The cold fear churned through his stomach and worked its way up into his throat.

"What . . . where are we going? Please, tell me what you're going to do."

"Please." One of the men haw-hawed. "Listen to 'im. He ain't such a big-shot editor now."

The horses were moving at a steady trot. Jones could see that they were on one of the streets behind his house and were going east into the mountains.

"Please, can't we discuss this? What are you going to do?" The fear made his voice tremble and his mind whirl.

"Haw-haw. Say please some more. I like to hear you say please."

He tried to control the fear, to stop his mind from spinning. Pleading was useless. They were determined. They were taking him somewhere into the mountains. Were they going to make it look like an accident? How could they hope to get away with it?

"Listen." He tried to think. "There has to be another way. You can't just kill me."

"Haw-haw. Go ahead, say, 'please'."

The horses slowed to a walk as they started up a steep grade, which Jones knew was just east of the town. What was up there? Mines? No, not in that direction. Where were they going?

"Why are you doing this? I can't believe you're doing this just to get even with me."

"Gettin' even? Haw-haw. Shit no, we're just gonna make you disappear, and then you won't be no trouble to nobody no more."

"Trouble? For who? What did I do?"

"It ain't what you done, it's what you might do."

"What?" He was genuinely curious now, and for the moment, at least, his mind was working. "What might I do?"

The other man said, "You ask too many damned questions, Mr. Editor."

"About what?"

"About . . . shit, you'll never know. You're gonna die without even knowin' why."

"Is that fair? I ought to know why you're doing this."

"Shut yer face." The man clucked at the team again and got them into a trot. "I ain't tellin' you a damned

220

thing."

"Why not? I've got a right to know why you want to kill me."

"It ain't me. If it was up to me I'd stomp the shit out of you and send you packin' back East where you come from."

"If not you, who?"

"Shut up. Shut yer damned face."

They rode in silence. Jones could hear the horses blowing through their nostrils as they labored. How far had they traveled? Four miles? Five? They were still going uphill, but it wasn't as steep here as it was just outside town. When the horses tried to slow down, one of the men cursed them and said, "Give me that whip. We got to git up there and git this over with."

The whip cracked and the buggy lurched forward at a greater speed. Jones tried to twist his wrists, but couldn't. His fingers were numb.

"It's about there. I can see that big pile of boulders right there. Here's where we quit the road."

"Hope these horses don't fall in a hole. There's more than one hole around here."

"Don't worry about that. They can see in the dark like a cat."

Holes? Prospectors' holes? Jones remembered seeing one of them. It was a hole dug by a prospector looking for precious metals. It was deep, and it was abandoned when no precious metals were found.

"I know they can see, but I don't want to take no chances. Let 'em slow down to a walk."

The buggy slowed. "We're almost there anyway."

The buggy bounced over rocks and tipped first to

one side and then the other. They were going across country now where there was no road.

"Hope the damned doubletree don't break. I'm damned if I wanta walk back."

"I think we're almost there."

"How do you know? I don't see anything."

The horses stopped suddenly. "What the hell're they stoppin' for?"

"I'm damned if I . . . oh, it's that down tree. We're right in front of it. We gotta turn south here."

"It's darker'n a black cat's ass." He clucked to the horses and swung the whip. "Turn around, you sonsofbitches." The buggy turned and moved forward again.

Jones strained his eyes, trying to see where they were, but the night was black. The bouncing vehicle threw him against the man on his right, and the man cursed. He fell next against the man on his left.

"Hold that sonofabitch off me."

"Hell, I got a better idee. Why don't I just shoot 'im. He won't be no trouble then."

"Yeah, nobody's gonna hear the shot now."

Ice suddenly formed around Jones's heart when he heard the sound of a pistol being cocked. He was about to be shot. He was about to die. He wanted to plead. Beg. He didn't want to die. His mouth opened, but no words came out. They were going to kill him right there.

"Wait just a minute. That damned cannon of yours might shoot right through 'im."

The man on his left said, "Whoa," and the buggy stopped. "Make shore I ain't in the way when you pull that trigger."

"You won't be if you bend down. I'll put 'er right up to his head."

Oh my God. Jones felt the end of the gun barrel against his right temple. His mind screamed, Don't. Don't. But his mouth only twisted wordlessly.

The man on his left bent down out of the way. Jones ducked down, too, trying to get away from the gun barrel. He wanted to fight, to do something. He was wedged in between them with his hands tied behind his back. He could do nothing.

"Dammit, don't shoot. The sonofabitch is right up against me. Don't shoot, dammit."

"Let's git the shithead out of here where we've got some room. The shot might spook the team anyway. These country horses ain't used to noise, and I'm damned if I want a busted singletree."

"We're almost there. When we git there you c'n shoot 'im all you want to."

The man on his left clucked at the team, and the buggy was moving again, bouncing over the rocks, tipping to the left and then to the right. Jones wondered whether the gun was still cocked and aimed at him. He turned his head and tried to see, but couldn't. The man on his right had bad breath. Whiskey breath.

"It's over there. I c'n see that bunch of aspen trees."

"Yeah, that's it. That's the one with all the rocks piled around it. Nobody'll find 'im down there."

A cruel chuckle came from Jones's right. "Not with all that rock on top of 'im."

"Whoa."

Were they going to put him in a hole with rocks on

223

top of him? That's it. That's what they had in mind. Shoot him, drop his body in one of those prospector's holes and cover his body with rocks. No one would find him there. No one would ever know what became of him.

A lantern was lighted, and the man on his right was pulling at him. "Come on, git out'n there. You're about to take your last steps, mister."

They were going to shoot him and dump his body in a deep hole. Icy fingers clutched at his chest.

"Walk 'im over here. No use carryin 'im."

He was pushed ahead. He stumbled over a rock and almost fell. A hand grabbed him by the hair and pulled at him.

"Stand up, mister. Take your medicine like a man."

Like a man. Sure. Just do as they say and die like a man. What would they think—Marybelle, Jake, and Mrs. Hansen? Would they think he just left town in the middle of the night? Of course not. They would know something happened. What would they tell his mother? Would the sheriff send her another telegram from Leadville saying her son had disappeared?

He was being pushed ahead toward a deep hole where he would be shot in the head. He stumbled again. Rough hands groped for him.

"Hold that light up. I don't wanta fall in that hole."

The lantern was raised. "Now I c'n see. Yep. It's right here. Won't take long to shovel these rocks down there."

A hand pulled at his bound wrists and pulled him to a stop. "Right here."

His mind screamed, Don't. His knees suddenly went weak, and he stumbled again. Rough hands

224

pulled at him. "Come on, git it over with."

His mind was screaming again. Run. Kick. Do something.

Jones ducked, whirled, hit the man behind him with his shoulder. The gun went off in his ear. He ran, feeling awkward with his hands bound behind him. Running like a girl. Run. Another shot. A hornet stung his right shoulder.

His feet were still moving. Run. Where? Get around to the other side of that buggy. Run. He ran into the buggy, fell back, got up and ran around it. The horses were snorting and stamping their feet. They didn't like the gunshots.

"Where'n hell is he?"

"He's over there by the horses. Don't shoot the horses."

Run, Will Jones. Run, you long, tall drink of water. Head for the darkest area you can find. Run like a girl, but run.

He was away from the buggy now, and he knew his footsteps could be heard. Gunfire came from behind him. Two shots. Another. Three more. He heard a bullet sing an angry song near his right ear. Another whined off a rock near his feet. Still another pulled at the left side of his shirt.

He stumbled and went down on his knees. A bullet zinged over his head. He rolled onto his feet and ran on.

"Dammit, where is he?"

"Right over there. Shoot over there."

Two more shots. He ran, stumbled, ran.

"Dammit, we gotta git 'im."

If only he could free his hands. He could run better

225

if he could use his arms for balance. Another shot.

Jones ran into the darkness, not knowing which direction he was running, not caring. Only trying to get away from those bullets. He ran, stumbled staggered, ran.

The ground dropped from under him. Something exploded in his head. Rocks scraped his arms and legs. His shirt was ripped from his back. He was falling.

Blackness covered him. Blacker than the night. Another bright light flashed through his brain.

He heard himself grunt, and that was all.

Chapter Twenty-seven

He wasn't aware of daylight coming. He wasn't aware of anything for a long time. The first thing he was aware of was the pain in his head. Awful pain. Thumping. Grinding. Hammering. A long, painful groan came out of him, and then he saw the redness.

Everything was red. He blinked, trying to clear his vision. The redness swirled, parted, and was replaced by a dark-gray, shapeless mass. He couldn't move his hands. Why couldn't he move his hands? Where was he?

He blinked again. There was light. Where was it coming from? Gradually, his vision cleared, and he looked around without turning his head. It hurt to turn his head. At first he couldn't make it out. Just a dark mass all around him.

Jones tried again to move his hands. It felt as if he had no hands. No hands and no arms. He groaned again and tried to turn his head. God, it hurt. Have to move it. Have to look up. With more groans and with clenched jaws, he turned his head and looked up. He knew then where he was.

It was one of those prospector's holes. Had to be.

Rock wall all around him. Jagged rock. He was sitting on his feet, and he tried to move them. Couldn't. Feet numb. Legs numb.

Got to move. How?

Concentrate. Move your right foot. Make it move. There. Now the left. Move, dammit. There. Now try your hands again. Nothing. No feeling at all. Tied? Of course. Now he remembered. All right, move your feet. Move. What a headache.

A cold sweat broke out on his forehead as he concentrated on moving his feet. Got to stand. He tried to wipe his face on his right shoulder. His shoulder hurt. Move feet.

At least his legs weren't broken. Couldn't move his feet if they were. Now got to stand. Come on, concentrate.

He managed to lean back against a rocky wall—fall back, rather. Now his feet were in front of him. He forced himself to pick up his right foot and then his left. His legs worked. Now stand up.

By pushing with his feet and bracing himself against the wall behind him, he moved. Slowly, an inch at a time, he got halfway up. His legs collapsed.

All right, rest awhile and try again.

Wonder if anyone will look for me. Of course they will. Marybelle will look for me. Marybelle and Jake. Can they find me? She's a tracker. Learned from her grandfather, and he could probably track a bird in flight. Played Indian tracking games as a child. She'll find me.

How long? Oh God, how my head hurts.

Pain, red dizzying pain, swarmed over him again, and he almost blacked out. Hurt all over. My legs, my shoulder, my side. Shirt nothing but rags.

When the pain subsided a moment, he tried again to stand. Inch by inch he forced his legs to push his back up the wall until finally, with sweat beaded on his face, he was upright. Now what?

If only he could free his hands. Free them? Hell, he couldn't even feel them. Ropes too tight, cutting off the blood circulation. How long could his hands live without blood? Were they permanently ruined?

And even if he could free his hands, he couldn't climb out. The top of the hole was at least six feet over his head. The rock wall was jagged, but there was nothing to get a finger hold on. Jagged? Yeah, sharp in places. Let's see.

He looked behind him, looked for a protruding rock with a sharp edge. Saw one.

With more grunting and groaning, he twisted his body so his hands were resting on the sharp edge. By looking over his shoulder he could see that they were. Now get the rope against the edge. He strained. The red pain was back. Red, blinding pain. Jones grunted and collapsed.

How long had he been here? What time of day was it? Would he ever get out or was he going to die here? He shook his head and blinked his eyes. Think. At least now he was sitting on the seat of his pants—on his ass where a man was supposed to sit. Stand up.

He got halfway up, and his knees folded. Now he was kneeling at the bottom of the hole. Try again. Oh God. All right, rest a minute and try again.

He tried to relax and rest and recover some

strength. Think about something else. What? Home? His mother? Naw, that just made him feel worse. Think about that train ride across the plains of Kansas and eastern Colorado.

"Goin' purt' near sixty mile an hour," the conductor had said. Jones couldn't believe it, though he knew he was traveling faster than he had ever traveled in his life. The tall prairie grass and sagebrush was going by so fast his eyes couldn't follow it.

"Easy to tell. What you do is you count the telegraph poles, see how many we pass in a minute. There's forty poles per mile, and if you count forty in a minute, then we're goin' sixty miles and hour."

Jones took out his watch, opened the lid, waited until the minute hand was on a minute marker, then started counting the poles. At the end of a minute he did some mental arithmatic and calculated they were going about fifty-five miles an hour. He shook his head in wonderment. Man wasn't meant to travel that fast.

All right, try. His legs were shaky and threatening to collapse any second, but Jones got himself up. He looked at the top. Would it do any good to yell for help? Of course not.

Come on, Marybelle. Please hurry.

And then he saw her.

Marybelle's face appeared over him. He couldn't believe it. She just appeared.

"Will?" She was looking down at him. She looked back over her shoulder and yelled, "Jake. He's here. He's alive." She was looking down at him again.

"Will, thank God. How badly are you hurt?"

His mouth opened, but only a squeak came out. He tried again and managed, "Don't know. Hands tied. Can't move them."

"Jake, hurry up." Then Jake's face was beside hers, looking down at him. "You're alive, boss. Hallelujah, you're alive."

"Jake, bring that rope on my saddle. I've got to get down there and help him. He's hurt."

Jake disappeared and reappeared. A half-inch rope was lowered into the hole, and Jones watched the end of it fall at his feet. Marybelle was sliding down the rope. She was carrying something in her teeth. A knife. She was beside him, her beautiful brown eyes searching his face, his body. "We're going to get you out of here, Will. You're going to survive."

He mumbled, "Marybelle, you're beautiful."

She was behind him with the knife. He saw his hands fall at his sides. He tried to move them, but couldn't.

She was rubbing his wrists and hands, rubbing vigorously. "Try to move your fingers, Will." He tried. "All right, move one finger." She picked up his left hand and held his forefinger out. "Move this one."

Sweat broke out on his face again as he tried. The finger jerked.

"Do you feel anything?"

"Uh. No, I, uh . . . there. I felt something."

"Try this one." She held out another finger. He tried. It moved. "How does that feel?"

"Like someone stuck a needle in it."

"That's good. The blood is circulating. Pretty soon it will hurt like the devil. Try to move all your

231

fingers."

She was right. A thousand hot needles were pricking his fingers, his hands, his wrists. It felt wonderful.

"Now we're going to get you out of here."

Working fast, so fast that he was only vaguely aware of what she was doing, she had the rope looped around both legs, up next to his crotch, up his back, around both shoulders, and tied there with a knot that wouldn't slip.

"You got it, Marybelle." It was Jake, looking down. "Can you climb out?"

She climbed the rope, hand over hand, using her feet to get toe holds against the rocky wall. Jones could see up her long skirt and the white petticoat, could see her tan legs. Beautiful legs.

"All right, boss, you're comin' out."

He could see Mahoney's stocky legs spread wide, close to the top of the hole, saw him bend his knees, pass the rope over his broad back near his shoulders and straighten his knees, pulling up. Marybelle took hold of the rope below Mahoney and pulled with both hands. He was lifted off his feet.

Mahoney grunted and strained, slipping the rope across his back as he pulled, Jones tried to help. First with his hands, but they had no strength, then with his toes.

Marybelle had hold of his shoulders, pulling. Her teeth gleamed against her dark skin as she strained.

"Grab hold of my legs, boss."

He managed to wrap his arms around Mahoney's left leg and hang on. Mahoney had him by the belt and lifted him up, lifted him as though he were a bundle of rags.

He was on the ground, gasping. Marybelle was on her knees beside him. "Stay still. Let's have a look."

She immediately found the knife wound in his left side and the bullet wound in his right shoulder.

"He's been shot," Mahoney said.

"Yes, but the bullet went through. It didn't hit any bone. We need some antiseptic and some bandages."

Her cool hand was turning his head. She sucked in her breath. "Oh my. This is a nasty one. This is going to take some sutures."

"Godamighty, boss, that musta knocked you out like a light on Saturday night."

Grinning weakly, Jones said, "I thought I was dead. Maybe I am. You two sure look like angels to me."

"You obviously hit your head when you fell into that hole, Will."

"That hole saved my life. They were shooting at me." He got his hands in the dirt and pushed himself to a sitting position. "If they'd waited until daylight they would have found me before you got here. How did you find me?"

"It was Marybelle, boss. We went lookin' for you, and she read the ground in front of your house like it was twenty-four point Bodoni Bold. She got her horse, and I borried one from Mrs. Hansen, and she led the way right here. I mean, boss, she didn't waste a step."

"But how . . . there were two men running all over, looking for me and shooting at me."

She touched one of his torn patent leather shoes. "You leave tracks that are easy to identify."

Jones smiled a real genuine, happy smile. "You're

wonderful. Both of you." The smile faded. "Now I've got to get up."

It was easier than he thought it would be. His knees were weak and his right shoulder was sore but he was standing, and he was swinging his arms and clenching and unclenching his fists.

"My horse will carry double," Marybelle said.

"Then let's go back to town. I've got things to do."

Chapter Twenty-eight

Jones refused to go see the doctor. In spite of Marybelle's urging he insisted on going first to the office of town marshal Waller Vaughn. "Those two hoodlums are not local," he said. "I'm sure of that from the things they said. And I don't know whether one of them owned the team and buggy, but I have the impression they don't. I can't identify the horses and buggy because it was too dark to see them clearly, but I can identify one of the men. Louis Eddman. I got a look at his face when he struck a match." Jones knew he was a bloody, ragged mess, but right then he didn't care. His strength came from the anger he felt and his determination to find those responsible for his anger.

"If they don't own the team and buggy, then they borrowed it from somebody, is that it, Will?"

"That's right, and if we can catch them we might make them tell who."

"And if they had to borrow transportation last night, then they're planning on leaving town by another means. The stage, maybe."

"Right again, and that explains why they didn't wait until daylight to look for me up there."

Marybelle nodded in agreement. "They had to get the horses and buggy back to town before daylight so they wouldn't be seen, and they have to get out of town as soon as possible."

Waller Vaughn was in his office, and he listened to what Jones had to say. He, too, thought the tall young man ought to see the doctor, but he didn't press the point.

Instead he pulled a watch out of a shirt pocket, glanced at it and said, "The stage is leaving in about half an hour. Come on, let's get over there."

But they were disappointed. Only two passengers boarded the stage, and they were both women.

"Then they had other means of transportation," Jones said. "They could have had saddle horses, I guess."

"Or," Marybelle added, "they could have traveled by freight wagon."

"Yeah." Waller Vaughn rubbed his chin and looked down at his boots. "There's freight wagons leavin' every day. Let's see, now." He continued rubbing his chin. "If any have left this mornin' they came from the smelter or from one of the stores. Let's get over to the smelter."

Jones's right shoulder was getting stiff, and he was holding his arm up at waist level to alleviate some of the pain. His head was throbbing again.

They went on horseback to the smelter. Mahoney stayed behind so Jones could ride the horse he had borrowed. Waller Vaughn was mounted on a handsome buckskin. It was the first time Jones had been close to the smelter, and he was surprised at how large it was. The smelter consisted of four buildings made of corrugated sheet metal, and one of the buildings covered two acres of ground. A tall smokestack came out of that one. Another building had a large padlock on the door, and a man holding a shotgun in the crook of his arm stood in front of it. High piles of mill tailings nearly filled a nearby ravine where it had been dumped.

They stayed on their horses and rode around, looking over the workmen who were pushing ore carts on rails into the largest building. One of them recognized Marybelle and said, "Miss Doobwah, what're you doin' around here?" His eyes flicked from the girl to Jones, stayed on him long enough to take in the bloody head and torn shirt, and went back to the girl.

"We're looking for someone, Franklin. Have you seen a gentleman by the name of Louis Eddman?"

The workman straightened his back and flexed his shoulders to get the cramps out. "Don't b'lieve I know 'im."

"Have there been any freight wagons leaving here this morning?"

"Yeah. One's haulin' empty. Goin' up to Leadville to get some coke for the furnace, I reckon."

"Were there any passengers?"

"Yeah, Miss Doobwah, there was old Satchelfoot Gipson, the teamster, and there was a couple a other gents I never seen before."

"When did they leave?"

The workman's forehead wrinkled and he squinted at her. "Boy, you're fulla questions this mornin', Miss Doobwah. You mad at somebody?"

"Yes, Franklin, I am. We suspect those two men tried to kill Mr. Jones last night."

"No." His face registered surprise, and his eyes went back to studying Jones.

237

"Did one of them have a full beard?"

"Both of 'em did. And . . ." His face screwed up in concentration again. "Come to think of it I might of seen one of 'em around here before, but I don't know who he is."

Jones and Waller Vaughn looked at each other, and Jones said, "It's them. I'd bet anything. We have to get after them."

The marshal shook his head. "If they're on that wagon, they're out of town and out of my jurisdiction. You'll have to get the sheriff."

"The sheriff won't do anything."

Marybelle reined her horse around beside the marshal's buckskin. "Mr. Vaughn, would you tell us something? Would you tell us what you think of Sheriff Schmitt?"

"Well . . ." Waller Vaughn looked down and ran his fingers through his horse's mane. "I don't like to tell tales out of school, miss."

"You don't trust him either." Her eyes were locked onto his and didn't waver. He tried to look up, but couldn't meet her gaze.

The workman watched and listened, then remembered he was supposed to be working, and grunted and strained to get his ore cart moving again. " 'Scuse me, folks, but I got to tram this stuff to that jaw crusher in there."

Jones spoke as much to himself as to anyone else. "The sheriff was elected, but it's well known everywhere that whoever the town fathers want elected gets elected."

"Yeah." Waller Vaughn looked up at Jones, "The town honchos ballyhooed for him and got him

238

elected."

"And you don't trust him." Marybelle was still trying to read the marshal's face. The buckskin shuffled its feet and pulled at the bit, wanting to move on.

"Aw, old Schmitt just does what he's told to do."

"You don't think he's a crook?"

"He knows what he has to do to keep his job, that's all."

"And what he has to do," Marybelle said matter-of-factly, "is jump when the town fathers tell him to."

The marshal grinned at that and nodded his head in agreement.

"Has he ever killed anyone?" Jones asked.

"Naw. Not that I ever heard of. That deputy of his might. I wouldn't trust him any further than I could throw him up the side of that mountain over there. But old Omar, he's just a bunch of wind."

Jones pondered that, then asked, "Have you any idea why they came looking for us a couple of days ago?"

"When? Oh, I heard about that. I heard you popped a couple of caps at 'em."

"Did what?"

"Fired a couple of shots."

"Yes, but I didn't intend to hit anyone."

"Well, I can only guess. I'd guess that somebody saw the two of you ride out of town, and when you didn't come back right away, they sent old Omar and his sidekick to try to find out what you were up to. Say, what were you up to, anyway?"

"We'll tell you, Mr. Vaughn, but not just yet."

"They knew you weren't prospectin' 'cuz you didn't

239

have any tools with you."

Jones chuckled dryly. "You can't move around here much without everyone knowing about it."

Waller Vaughn grinned again. "I'm guessin' old Schmitt didn't learn much."

"He's already learned what to do and what not to do," Jones said, "and he is not going to go after those two men."

The doctor was young, thin, with a clean-shaven face and bushy dark hair. He shaved the side of Jones's head, took six stitches in the wound and apologized for not having a stronger anesthetic. Jones gritted his teeth and managed to keep quiet.

The bullet wound high on Jones's upper right arm was cleaned and bandaged, and the doctor insisted that he carry the arm in a sling. It would be better if he didn't move the arm. The knife wound in his left side was shallow, and it, too, was cleaned and bandaged.

Marybelle accompanied Jones to his house where he closed the bedroom door and put on some clean clothes while she mixed some pancake batter and fried some bacon.

"At least my jaw isn't sore anymore." Jones grinned a lopsided grin as he ate.

"You've had a terrible time of it, Will. Why don't you lie down and rest."

"I can't, Marybelle. This thing has gone on too long. It's got to stop. I've got to stop it."

"We have to stop it, Will."

He grinned at her. "You bet."

She poured another cup of black coffee. "We learned one thing this morning. If those two passengers on the freight wagon are your antagonists, then Mr. Pope is definitely part of the plot."

"Yeah, but we suspected that all along. The problem is how to prove it." Eating with his left hand was awkward at first, but Jones soon got the feel of it, and he cleaned his platter.

"There's only one way." Marybelle put her coffee cup down. "Find the gold."

"Yeah. If Pope has it, and we both think he has, it's got to be somewhere inside one of those buildings at the smelter. And since it was stolen from the U.S. Mint at Denver, it ought to be easy to identify."

Marybelle was quiet, her eyes half closed. Then she looked up. "We are convinced now that Mr. Pope is a crook, but something bothers me."

He waited for her to go on.

"We know . . . everyone knows . . . there are four or five men who run the town of Maxwell. Mr. Pope is one of them. Are the others involved?"

"Well now." Jones took a quick sip of coffee. "Let's think about this. How could the others be involved?"

Her eyes were half closed again. Jones said, "None of them are the kind to be armed robbers. Unless the deputy sheriff is involved, and somehow I don't think he is."

"Why, Will?"

"He's just not in the class with the others. I mean men like John Pope, Josef Grunenwald, Wilbur Osgood, Cyrus Dochstader, Oliver Scarbro: They're all men of means—businessmen—while the deputy is a hired hand."

241

"How would those five men you named get their hands on some stolen gold? Buy it?"

"Sure." Jones sat up straighter in his chair. "That's how they got it."

"Uh-huh." Her eyes were fixed on his. "Suppose, just suppose, the hoodlums who stole the gold found themselves with something they didn't expect. Suppose they thought they were stealing money, and when they opened the crates, or whatever, they found themselves with a ton of gold on their hands. What would they do with it?"

Jones chuckled. "They sure couldn't buy a drink in a saloon with it. They couldn't buy a house with it, and they couldn't buy a ticket to South America."

"So." Marybelle'e eyes were alive, dancing. "They had to sell it to someone who could spend it, and that someone was John Pope."

"I think we've got it, Marybelle. I don't know how these five gentlemen got acquainted with the thieves— through a relative or a common acquaintance—but somehow they did, and they bought the stolen gold for, say, fifty cents on the dollar or forty cents or maybe less."

"And," she added, "that took a lot of cash, more probably than any one or two men in Maxwell could raise, so the five pooled their cash, bought the gold and shipped it here in wooden crates disguised as mining equipment or merchandise."

"And," he continued the thought, "now they're remelting it, and doubling their investment. Or more than doubling it."

Marybelle stood, smiling. Then the smile disappeared and she sat down again. "And now we're back

242

to the problem of trying to prove it."

"Yeah." Jones's enthusiasm vanished, too. "If, as you said, we could find the gold in their possession, that would be pretty good proof. But how can we do that?"

They were quiet, each deep in thought.

"I guess," Jones said resignedly, "the only thing we can do is go to Leadville, hunt up the district attorney, try to make him believe what we believe, and try to persuade him to get a search warrant. That gold has to be out there in one of those buildings at the smelter."

"Yes, I'm sure it's there. I saw a small steel building that was locked and guarded. I've heard it said that Mr. Pope goes in there every morning with a small wooden box and comes out with the same box, then goes into the main building where the furnace is."

"That's where it is then. Thomas Jackson told me about that building. I saw it when we were over there, not more than two hours ago."

"I saw it, too."

"There's gold in it, gold stolen from the U.S. Mint in Denver."

She sat with her chin in her hands. "Padlocked and guarded."

"Dynamite couldn't break it open." Suddenly Jones sat up straight again. "Or could it?"

She looked at him curiously. "I suppose it could. Certainly enough dynamite could. Why?"

"Oh, I don't know. I just got a crazy idea. It's crazy."

"Will." Marybelle wore a frown. "You're not thinking about . . . that would be illegal."

"All right, so it's illegal. It's either that or go to the district attorney, and I don't know whether he would believe us and whether he would, or could, get a search warrant, and even if he did it would take several days, and I don't know about you, Marybelle, but I'm getting damned—darned—tired of all that's been going on, and I want to put a stop to it."

"So do I, Will. Believe me, I do. But . . . it's opposed to what you've been saying, what you've printed in the newspaper. It's taking the law into your own hands."

"All right." He was on the defensive. "But there are times when . . ." He didn't know what else to say, and he let his voice trail off.

She stared at him, puzzled, and suddenly she chuckled. "It's Indians like me who are supposed to go on the warpath, not gentlemen like you."

He chuckled with her but said nothing, and eventually they fell silent again. Jones got up from the table and paced the room. He rubbed his left hand over the stubble of beard on his chin, smoothed his moustache, fingered the bandage on his head. "Let's go see Justus DeWolfe. He's honest and he doesn't like the clique, as he calls them. Maybe he'll have a suggestion.

Chapter Twenty-nine

The lawyer's feet came off his desk, and he stood when Marybelle and Jones entered his office. Jones anticipated his first remark and explained how he happened to be wearing so many bandages. Then, as he and Marybelle sat in wooden chairs in front of the desk, he told the lawyer everything. DeWolfe's mouth opened, and his eyebrows went up as he listened without interrupting. When Jones finished talking, the lawyer smiled.

"It just happens I was over at your office an hour ago with some news, and you weren't there. You're looking at the newly appointed deputy district attorney of Maxwell County. I've got a job."

"What?" Jones looked at Marybelle. Marybelle looked at Jones.

"Congratulations," Jones said. "That's good news. In fact, that's very good news. We were just thinking of going to Leadville and hunting up the DA. Now we can turn it over to you."

But the lawyer was shaking his head negatively. "No. I'd certainly like to handle this case, but I can't. Stealing from the U.S. Mint is a crime against the federal government, and the U.S. Attorney is the prosecutor."

"Aw damn." Jones apologized to Marybelle. "Darn, I mean."

"Damn is right," she said. "I feel the same way."

"We just seem to be frustrated at every turn." Jones pounded his knee in frustration. "We know damn well what's going on here, and we can't do anything about it."

"Yes, we can." DeWolfe crossed his arms on top of his desk. "It will take some time, of course. What I can do—will do—is go to Leadville and fire off a wire to the U.S. Attorney in Denver. He'll be tickled to death to get the news, and he'll send some marshals here, and some of those marshals are hardcases themselves. They'll get to the bottom of this. And I'll alert the Leadville police and the Denver police to be on the lookout for this Louis Eddman. Him, I can prosecute."

"Sure, sure." Jones shifted in his chair and studied the floor. "Time. That's something we haven't got much of." He looked up at the lawyer. "John Pope can't help but suspect we're onto him. He knows we're onto something or he wouldn't have sent those to hoodlums to kill me. He'll move the gold so we'll never find it. Without it we have no case."

Marybelle shifted in her chair, too, uncrossed and recrossed her legs under the long skirt. "Can't you at least get a search warrant?"

DeWolfe pursed his lips. "I don't know. I can try, but I can make no promises. The state district judge might refuse to meddle in federal affairs. But I can try."

They were silent. Marybelle studied her hands folded in her lap. Jones looked down at his torn patent leather shoes without seeing them. DeWolfe stared at a spot on the wall over Jones's head. Then Jones said, "All right, so robbing the mint is a federal crime, but how about murder?"

"Murder?" The lawyer's gaze came down from the wall and centered on Jones's face.

"Yes, murder. We're convinced that my uncle, Nathan Benchley, was murdered. And I've been thinking, too, about that accident that killed Bertrum Hansen."

They told the lawyer about it. Jones did most of the talking, but Marybelle filled in some of the details. When they finished, the lawyer started shaking his head again. Jones felt like yelling at him to quit shaking his head and do or say something positive for a change.

"It won't hold up in court. I can't even get an arrest warrant on that kind of evidence."

"But it's as clear as anything. At least to Marybelle and her grandfather. And I can even name one of the killers. Or, a man I'm almost certain was one of them. Louis Eddman."

"We just have no real evidence."

Now Jones was angry. "Aw damn."

"There is hope," the lawyer said. "Once the marshals get through with John Pope and company they'll know a lot more about this whole mess. And if Mr. Benchley was murdered because of this mess, they'll find out about that, too. And if they give me anything to go on, anything at all, I'll prosecute the h—heck out of them."

"If they get their hands on Louis Eddman . . . I've got a hunch he's a weak man. Psychologically, that is. He might be the weak link in the chain. Another possible weak link is Sheriff Omar Schmitt.

"I'll tell them that."

"But in the meantime, will you do something, Mr. DeWolfe, something that might be against your principals but is very important."

"What might that be?"

"Be at the Bijou Smelter and Reduction Works tonight. At nine o'clock."

"But why?"

"Just be there. You don't have to do anything else. I need you as a witness."

The lawyer put his elbows on the desk and made a steeple of his fingers. "Are you going to tell me what this is all about?"

"No. But if you're the kind of man I think a deputy DA ought to be, you'll be there. I promise, your career will not be jeapordized."

"Um." He put his lips to his fingertips. "I won't do anything illegal."

"I'm not asking you to. Will you be there?"

"All right."

"Can I count on you?"

"Yes. I'll be there."

"Bring a lantern, but don't light it until you get my signal."

Marybelle had to half run at times to keep up with Jones's long-legged strides as they hurried to the office of Waller Vaughn. The town marshal was reset-

248

ting a shoe on his buckskin gelding, and when he saw them approaching he let the horse's left forefoot down and straightened his knees and back slowly, painfully.

"This sonofagun stands still while I work on his feet, but he leans over on me," he said conversationally. "And b'lieve me when an eleven hundred pound horse leans on you you know you're bein' leaned on. What've you two got on your minds this time?"

Jones asked him to be at the smelter at nine P.M.

"What for?" The marshal's eyes narrowed. "What're you up to?"

"I can't tell you. But something is going to happen. I promise you won't be disappointed."

Waller Vaughn eyed him suspiciously for a moment, then his mouth twisted into a wry grin. "Now you've got me curious."

"Will you be there?"

"I'll be there, and that's a promise."

"Bring a lantern."

Their next stop was the newspaper office. "I wondered where you two was," Mahoney said. "What's been goin' on?"

Jones didn't answer immediately and instead picked up a letter that had come in the mail that morning. It was from Nathaniel Martin of Denver. Jones read it and frowned. "Mr. Martin wants to open a new store here," he said to his employees, "but he got some discouraging news from the mayor about the price of lots and the high rents. He did say, however, that if the situation changes he will open a store as soon as possible, and he asked me to keep him informed."

"There ain't no aces in buyin' a lot here, boss."

"What makes me see red," Jones muttered aloud, "is the way the city council publicly welcomed him but privately discouraged him. They sang two different songs."

"They're trying to hold onto their little monopoly," Marybelle said.

"Yeah. That's got to stop. That, among other things." He turned to his printer, who was wearing his paper hat on the back of his head. "Jake, do you know anything about dynamite?"

"Wall, I dunno. I seen it used. I guess I do. Why?"

"I want you to go over to the mercantile and buy some. I don't know how much. Enough to blow a big hole in a steel shed."

Mahoney's mouth dropped open in astonishment. "Boss, what're you gonna do?"

"Will you do that?"

"Wal, sure, if that's what you want. If it's dynamite, prob'ly three sticks oughta do it."

"Get everything it takes." Jones reached for his hip pocket. "Here's some money."

"You're the dealer." Mahoney hitched up his baggy wool pants and left.

"You're going to do it." Marybelle slid into the barrel chair while Jones plopped down at his desk.

"Yes, Marybelle. I know it's illegal, but I just have to do something."

"You could be arrested and put back in jail."

"I know."

"What's worse, you could blow yourself up. You've had no experience with explosives."

"I know."

"But you're going to do it."

"What do you think I should do, Marybelle?"

"I certainly can't advise you to do anything like this. But . . ." She shook her head sadly. "I know how you feel. I feel the same way."

"Then you don't blame me?"

She didn't answer. Instead, she said quietly, seriously, "Be careful, Will."

Mahoney showed him how to do it. "I got three sticks, boss, and three feet of fuse and a blastin' cap. I borried it from a miner friend of mine instead of buyin' it at the store. I didn't want to tip your hole card, whatever it is."

"That's good."

"Here's what you do, boss." Mahoney tied the three sticks together with a piece of string. "You got a knife? It only takes a little one."

"I've got a penknife, yes."

"What you do is, you cut a slit in this middle stick, right here, see. Then you cut a piece of fuse. Give yourself plenty. You put the end of the fuse in this little sleeve here in this blastin' cap, see."

"Uh-huh." Jones watched and listened intently.

"Be mighty careful with this cap, boss. It ain't as powerful as a stick of dynamite, but if it goes off in your hand it'll take some fingers off. Got it?"

"Uh-huh. What's it for?"

"It's to set off the powder. It takes a little explosion to set off the big one, see, but it ain't so little. Be mighty careful with it."

"Uh-huh."

"Now, you have to crimp the sleeve of this here cap onto the fuse so it'll stay put. Use a pair of pliers. I seen a man crimp one with his teeth once, but he was crazy. He done it one time too many and when we berried him we wasn't right sure who we berried, but nobody done seen him anymore so it musta been him. Now then, you push this here cap with the fuse on it into the slit you cut in this middle stick. Then you light the fuse and git. And, boss, give yourself enough fuse that you can walk away. Don't run. If you run you might trip and fall."

"I got it."

"You sure? You sure you got the rights of it? Men've been killed with this stuff."

"I'll be careful. How much fuse do you think I'll need?"

"DamfIknow. But if I was drawin' to this hand I'd use ever' inch of what I got here."

"All right."

Chapter Thirty

They had nothing to set in type, and Jones and Marybelle went to her house for lunch. They considered the Hansen House, but Jones didn't want to talk about the attempt on his life and his night in a prospector's hole.

It was the first time Jones had been in Marybelle's house, and it made him ashamed of his housekeeping. Everything was clean and neat. The rugs on the floor were handmade of Angora wool, made with colorful Indian craftsmanship. The furniture was cushioned and comfortable. The kitchen had a bank of handmade cabinets, a wooden table with a polished top, a porcelain sink, a short-handled pump, and a four-lid, wood-burning stove with an oven. A lid-lifter hung on a hook near the stove.

She served him homemade potato soup and homemade dark bread with butter that she had bought from a neighbor. It was even better than the meals served at the Hansen House. After they ate, she washed the dishes, and they sat on the cushioned sofa in the living room. He wondered what her bedroom was like, but he couldn't think of a tactful way to find out.

"Will, I'd like to talk to you about something. This may not be the best time, and I'm not at all sure you'll agree with what I'm proposing. If you don't, I'll understand."

The meal felt good in his stomach, and he doubted he could ever disagree with anything she said. "Try me."

She half turned on the sofa, facing him. "I'd like to own an interest in *The Maxwell Times*."

"Huh?"

I have some money that Mr. Tucker left me, and I want to own something. Your uncle, Mr. Benchley, was a dedicated journalist, and working with him got me interested in journalism, too."

When he didn't answer immediately, she went on. "I know I don't have the education you have, but I've been trying to learn to write. I've been practicing writing news, and I can learn."

"Uh, Marybelle." He stroked his moustache. "You can write just fine. Better than I can. It's just that, uh . . ." He didn't know what to say. It was something that required some thought.

She turned away from him and faced the far wall. "It was just an idea. I understand. I'm sorry I mentioned it, especially at a time like this."

But he could see the disappointment in her, and he didn't want to disappoint her. He didn't want to hurt her in any way. "You know," he said, speaking carefully, "when this mess is over, and I believe it soon will be, this town is going to grow. *The Times* will have to grow with it. I know where we can buy a rotary press second hand. Whatever that is. Jake will

254

know. And . . . I don't have a lot of money left."

She turned back, facing him again, eyes leveled at him.

"Marybelle, if you want to, if you're sure you want to, I'd be happy to have you as a partner."

Her smile was contagious, and he smiled, too.

"And you're the editor, reporter, writer, and anything else you want to be. I'll be business manager, and, uh . . ." He grinned. "Printer's devil."

A frown appeared, vanished, and her entire face was smiling. "You'll always be the boss."

"Oh no. We're equal partners, and I mean equal in every way."

They talked and made plans, and she was as excited as a child with a new toy. Her excitement rubbed off on him, and he forgot everything else and was just happy to see her so happy.

"I know how a rotary press works," she said. "Jake described it to me. It had two cylinders. You can lock the type faces on each cylinder and roll the paper between them. You can print both sides of the paper at the same time. It's much faster than a flatbed press."

At mid-afternoon his eyelids were becoming heavy, and she persuaded him to lie down on her bed. While she unlaced and removed his shoes, he enjoyed the feel of the crocheted coverlet and the pillow that smelled of her. With his good hand he tried to pull her down on the bed with him, but she smilingly resisted, and after she left the room he realized she was right. This was not the time and he was not in condition.

He slept with a smile on his face. There would be other times.

And then she was shaking him awake. "It's almost dark, Will. I'll have supper on the table soon."

For a moment, after he awakened, he didn't know what it was he was supposed to do. He had an overpowering feeling there was something he had to do, and it took a moment to remember. The remembrance, when it came, settled on him like a dark cloud of impending danger.

He had to blow up a building.

Chapter Thirty-one

Marybelle wanted to go with him. "I'm an expert stalker. When I was a child we played stalking games as well as tracking games. No one can stalk like an Indian."

"I don't doubt for a minute that you can sneak up behind that shed a lot quieter than I can, Marybelle. And your tracking skills saved my life. But please let me do this myself. I'd never forgive myself if you went along with my crazy scheme and got hurt."

She studied his face, then said quietly, "All right, Will."

He had it planned. He'd have to go around to the east side of the smelter and come up behind the shed. The guard would be in front of it. If he worked quietly he could lay the dynamite and light the fuse without being heard or seen.

It was another black night with no moon, and Jones didn't dare use a lantern or even strike one of the wooden matches he carried in a shirt pocket. In another shirt pocket was the blasting cap, which Mahoney had given him. Jones carried the dynamite and fuse in his one good hand as he walked in the dark. When he reached the steep hill on the east side of town, he turned north and tried to see the buildings. Rocks made walking in his city shoes uncomfortable, and he wished he had gotten around to buying some new shoes—boots, rather. He stumbled over rocks and mountain shrubbery and worked his way north along the bottom of the hill.

Once he stumbled and fell onto his hands and knees, but instead of worrying about skinned knees he worried about the blasting cap he carried in his shirt pocket. Mahoney had warned him about blasting caps. It didn't take much to explode them. Carrying it in his shirt pocket was risky, but he had to carry it somewhere.

The fall made him realize he had to have two hands for the job, and he took his right arm out of the sling. The free movement of his arm brought a sharp pain from the bullet wound in his shoulder, and he decided he would have to use the sling again as soon as possible.

Where were the damned buildings? Even as dark as it was he ought to be able to see a dim outline of them. Or something. Funny thing about the mountains; when there was a full moon you could almost read a newspaper by the moonlight, and when there was no moon the night was totally black. Where in hell was he? He couldn't get lost, could he? Was that a building in front of him or was it a big spruce?

He picked his steps carefully. It wouldn't do to fall down this close to the smelter. Might alert the guard. Yes, it was a building. It was a small one, but not the one he was looking for.

He tried to visualize the way the smelter was laid

out—several small buildings and a big one. The locked shed was close to the big one, between it and some of the other buildings.

Jones groped his way slowly, trying to see in the dark, trying to find his target. He heard a voice. A man's voice. Threatening.

"Stop. Stop right there or I'll shoot."

Jones stopped. He looked around, his heart beating very fast. The voice came from the dark somewhere in front of him, but not nearby. Then he heard Marybelle.

"It's me. Marybelle Dubois. Don't shoot, Thomas."

"Marybelle? What in thunderation are you doin' here?"

Eyes straining, Jones finally saw her, or something that could be her. What he saw was a white blob in the dark about fifty feet away. The white blob moved and Marybelle said, "Don't shoot, Thomas."

"Marybelle, it can't be you. What in thunderation are you doin' around here?"

"There's something I have to tell you, Thomas. Something very important, but I can't see you clearly. Would you come over here?"

"What's goin' on, Marybelle? What are you doin'? Is somethin' wrong with Mrs. Hansen? What're you doin' here?"

Jones felt like asking the same questions. What in hell was she doing? Oh. Of course. The white dress made her easy to see in the dark, and she was drawing the guard away from the shed, making his chore easier. But, dammit, she could have been shot. Good thing the guard knows her. Well, what are you waiting for, you long, tall drink of water.

He could hear them talking, but he paid no attention to what they were saying as he groped his way to the back of the shed. Where to put it? He groped with his hands and discovered a rock foundation under the sheet metal and a spot where the corner of a sheet of corrugated steel had come loose. That would be a good place.

Working by feel, he used his penknife to cut a slit in the center of the stick of dynamite, then fitted the end of the fuse into the sleeve of the blasting cap. Got to crimp the sleeve with a pair of pliers, Mahoney said. Damn. Forgot the pliers. Would the fuse stay put without crimping? No, dammit. Got to crimp it. How? With my teeth? Oh no. If the damn thing went off it would take my head off. Goddamn. Whoops. This is not the time to use God's name in vain. Excuse me, Lord.

Carefully, Jones put the cap in his mouth. With his tongue for a feeler, he made certain he had the sleeve between the upper and lower molars on his left side, and carefully, ever so carefully, he bit down. Easy now. Easy. If it went off he wouldn't feel a thing. He wouldn't even know it. He'd never know anything again.

Easy. He felt the sleeve bend a little under the pressure. There. That ought to do it. He couldn't help breathing a sigh of relief when he took the cap, fuse and all, out of his mouth. Now, let's see, push the cap into the slit in the stick of dynamite. He was surprised at how soft the explosive was inside the paper tube. Like fine sand. Easy. There.

He listened and could hear Marybelle and the

guard talking, could hear her telling him, "Your boss, Mr. Pope, is a crook, Thomas. Something is going to happen, and I don't want you involved. We're friends, and I just had to warn you."

Jones could see her white dress clearly now, but the man was only a dark shadow. They were about forty feet in front of the building, out of danger. The man was arguing.

"Sure, we're friends, Marybelle, but I got a job to do. I can't stand here talkin' to you, and what is goin' on anyway? I never knowed you to do anything like this before. You've always been a perfect lady, and . . ."

Jones struck a wooden match on the sole of his left shoe and lit the fuse. He hoped the man wouldn't see the flare of light. The fuse sizzled. It was time to leave.

Walk, don't run. That was good advice, especially for a man moving about in the dark. He walked, stepping carefully so he wouldn't trip over anything. He hooked his thumb inside his belt to ease the pain in his right shoulder and got back to the bottom of the hill just before the explosion.

Chapter Thirty-two

It was the loudest noise he had ever heard—so loud it rocked his head. The concussion knocked him onto his knees, and he thought his eardrums had burst.

For a moment everything was quiet.

Then men were shouting, running. He saw a lantern bobbing in the night as someone carried it toward the ruined shed. Another lantern followed that one.

"Who's there?" It was Thomas Jackson's voice, high and nervous. "Stop or I'll shoot."

The next voice was Marybelle's. "Don't shoot, Thomas. Believe me it's in your best interest to put the gun down. Don't shoot anyone."

Then the marshal's voice, loud and commanding: "It's Marshal Waller Vaughn. I'm on official business."

Jones got back to the shed in time to see Waller Vaughn hold his lantern up and inspect the damage. The shed had been knocked off its foundation, and a sheet of metal was torn half off, forming a hole big enough for a man to stoop down and duckwalk through.

"Is that you, Jones?" The marshal held his lantern close to Jones's face.

"Yeah, it's me."

"Did you do this?"

"Yeah. There's something inside there that you ought to see."

"What?"

"It's inside." He squatted and led the way. The interior of the shed was dark, and he had to wait for the marshal to stoop down and enter with his lantern. There were two wooden crates, waist high. "Hold your light over here, will you?"

Stenciled on the sides of the crates were the words: Mining Machinery Bijou Smelter And Reduction Works Maxwell, Colo.

"What the humped-up hell is this all about, Jones?"

"Wait." The lid of the first crate came off easily. It had been pried off before. The lantern was held higher.

"What do you see, Mr. Vaughn?"

"Gold bricks. So what? This is a gold smelter."

And then the uncertainty hit. Jones suddenly realized he could have made a mistake. He was only guessing, and now he wondered if he was wrong. If he was, he was in trouble with the law for damaging someone else's property, and he would be the laughing stock of Maxwell County. He couldn't be wrong, dammit.

His voice was weak with uncertainty when he said, "Look closer, Mr. Vaughn."

A long pause. A sick lump began forming in Jones's stomach. Finally:

"Well, I'll be damned."

"What do you see?"

"It's got U.S. Mint stamped on it."

"Whoo." He realized he had been holding his breath.

Another figure and another lantern came through the hole. It was Justus DeWolfe. Then another man came in, followed by Marybelle Dubois in her white, lacy dress.

"Everyone take a look," Jones said.

"You were right, Mr. Jones." The lawyer was excited. "It's here, just as you suspected."

"Well for . . ." Thomas Jackson let the hammer down on his shotgun. "How in hell did that get here?"

Gold ingots were picked up and examined. "The whole box is full of them," DeWolfe said.

"Where in hell did it come from?" the marshal asked.

DeWolfe answered, "From the Denver Mint. It was stolen in a robbery last January. How it got here is a long story, and I believe I know all about it."

There was shouting outside, and more faces looked through the hole. One of them belonged to Sheriff Omar Schmitt. "Hey, what's goin' on in there? Come out of there, all of you. This is the sheriff speaking."

Silently, slowly, they filed out. Jones put his right

arm back in its sling. Waller Vaughn stood next to the hole in the shed with his hands on his hips, his right hand close to the holstered pistol. "Nobody goes in there till I say so. We're in the town limits, Omar."

With his good hand, Jones picked up the marshal's lantern. "There's evidence of a crime in there."

"The hell you say."

DeWolfe held his lantern up to the sheriff's face. "You knew about it, didn't you, Mr. Schmitt. Answer me. I'm the deputy district attorney for Maxwell County now, and I'm asking you a question."

"I don't know nothin' about nothin'."

"Yes you do. You know what's in there, don't you."

Omar Schmitt's voice had lost its power. "I don't know nothin'."

"Oh yes you do, and you're gong to tell us all about it, aren't you."

Justus DeWolfe was talking like a man with authority, like a trial lawyer cross-examining a witness.

"I don't know nothin'."

"This town will be swarming with U.S. Marshals in a few days, Mr. Schmitt, and they'll get it out of you. You know all about this, and you know how Nathan Benchley died, don't you."

"I didn't have nothin' to do with that."

"But you know who did, don't you."

"I don't know nothin' and I ain't sayin' nothin'." The sheriff began backing away.

"Stop. Stand right there." DeWolfe shouted at Schmitt as if he were accustomed to giving orders. The sheriff stopped. "You've got guilt written all over

265

you, Mr. Schmitt."

"I ain't done nothin'."

More men came running up. Among them were John Pope and Oliver Scarbro. "What's going on here?" Pope yelled. "Who are all of you and what are you doing here?"

"They blowed a hole in your shed, Mr. Pope," Omar Schmitt answered.

"We found some very incriminating evidence," DeWolfe said.

"What . . ." John Pope didn't finish his question. His face looked white in the lantern light.

"You know what. You're in deep trouble. You and your cohorts." The lawyer turned to the gathering. "You've all seen the evidence. I want you to remember it. You will have to testify in court to what you just saw."

"Did you say somethin' about bein' a deputy DA?" Waller Vaughn was staring hard at him.

"Yes." DeWolfe fished a leather wallet out of his pants pocket, opened it and displayed a silver badge. "I have the power to make arrests, but I'll leave that up to you."

"You want me to arrest everybody?"

"No. Not now. Just don't let them leave town. I'll turn this case over to the U.S. Attorney, and he and his marshals will take over. But murder is a crime against the state, and it has precedence over robbery. I intend to investigate the death of one, Nathan Benchley, and the attempted murder of William Jones. Between the state, local, and federal investigators, we'll get to the bottom of this."

Jones was surprised at the way DeWolfe had taken command.

"You say Nathan Benchley was murdered?" Waller Vaughn was still staring at the lawyer. "You're agreein' with this editor feller?"

"I know the identity of one of the culprits, and the sheriff knows, too. Don't you, Mr. Schmitt?"

"I don't know nothin'."

"All right. We've done everything we can tonight," DeWolfe said. "I would advise all of you not to leave town. If you do you won't get far, and your leaving will be taken as an admission of guilt. I will go to Leadville tomorrow and start the wheels of justice turning."

DeWolfe started to leave, but stopped. "Mr. Vaughn, we're not making any arrests yet. But we will. Yes, indeed, we will."

"Nobody touches that gold in there," Waller Vaughn said. "Thomas Jackson, I'm deputizin' you to help me guard it."

"Yeah," Jackson said, weakly. Jones sensed that the guard hadn't fully realized what was happening. But he would, and when he did he would be a dedicated guard.

Jones took Marybelle by the arm, and together they walked away. Not until they were out of the lantern light and out of earshot of the others did either of them speak.

She couldn't contain her excitement. "You did it, Will. Your plan worked." She did a pirouette and gripped his good arm.

"*We* did it. It took the two of us."

They said nothing further until they were on the plank sidewalk. Jones chuckled. "Your first assignment as reporter, editor, and half owner of *The Maxwell Times* is one hell of a story—heck, I mean. It'll be the biggest story in Colorado this year, and it will go out over the telegraph to the big newspapers all over the country."

"Oh my, it's kind of scary. I mean, I've written one published news story in my life. Oh, I hope I can do justice to it."

He put his good arm around her shoulders and pulled her to him. "You can do it." They walked on with his arm around her.

Inside the office of *The Times* he lit a lamp with one hand and turned to face her. They were alone. "Look at me, Marybelle." He remembered to straighten his shoulders.

She looked at him, her brown eyes going from the bandage on his head and the scar above his right eye to the thin welt on his cheek; then to the arm in a sling, down to the ruined patent leather shoes and back up to his face.

"Would you . . ." He had to swallow a lump in his throat before he could go on. "W—would you take a thing like this to be your lawful wedded husband?"

Her brown eyes were round as they looked into his, then her arms were around his neck and her body was tight against him. The first kiss was short and sweet, and it was followed by a long emotional one.

268

Finally she leaned back. Her eyes were moist, and a tear rolled slowly down one cheek. He kissed each eye. She blinked back the tears and smiled. It was the most beautiful smile he had ever seen.

"You bet your bottom dollar I would."

THE SURVIVALIST SERIES ·
by Jerry Ahern